THE REUNION

A Supernatural Anthology

MARISA MOHI   KATHRYN TRATTNER

MARNIE VINGE   COLLETTE CARMON

Maw See Saw Creative, Inc.

Contents

The Reunion

Marisa Mohi

Brendan hopped out of the shower but couldn't stop sweating. He hadn't been this nervous in a long time.

He felt silly for feeling this way about seeing a woman, especially one he didn't know, and it wasn't like it was a real date or anything. But Liz had messaged him. She'd found him on Facebook and let him know she would be there. And it felt just like that night twenty years ago all over again.

Brendan had never actually met Liz. But he'd chatted with her on AIM and knew that she went to the school across town. They made so many plans to meet up over their senior year. He had never seen a full body picture, but Brendan could tell she was hot. Her away message made her seem like a poet. Her photo made her seem like an artist. He couldn't believe that she was single, and it felt really weird to him that she wasn't a popular girl at her school, and that she didn't have someone there.

But he didn't question. When you're lucky, you're lucky. And Brendan didn't want to look a gift horse in the mouth.

So even though they had tried to meet up at the mall or the diner, it always fell through. Either Brendan couldn't get a ride or the timing was off. It was in the days when cellphones were new and expensive and no high schooler had the cash to be sending text messages all over the place.

But then it finally seemed like everything was looking up. On the night of graduation, there was going to be a party down by the old trestle bridge. It was a relic, the sort of thing that wound up on postcards or that landscape painters put on a canvas to sell to tourists who wanted to see the real America. But it was also a place that all the kids from the city's two high schools met up to smoke pot and have sex.

Brendan remembered showing up with spiked hair and layered polo shirts with the collars popped, trying to look his best. He wanted to show Liz how cool he was, and hopefully lose his virginity. But that night was cursed. Or, at least, that's what everyone seemed to think. Because that was the night that Cody Dempsey died.

Brendan ran a towel over his head, wondering if he had time to dye his hair. He was going gray, and while he wasn't ashamed of it, he didn't know how Liz looked these days other than the profile pic from her Facebook. She seemed just as young as she was then. Women were like that though. It was all the skincare products and makeup. But did that mean that he needed to play catchup?

Ultimately, he decided not to dye his hair, mostly because there wasn't time. And because he felt that maybe he looked more mature going gray.

Brendan picked up his phone to see if there were any new messages from Liz. He'd been out of the dating game for so long, only to find himself there just in time for the twenty-year reunion. The divorce had been mutual enough, and he saw his kids on weekend, which was fine, even if they weren't overly excited to come to his apartment.

And even though he thought the apartment downtown was cool, he had no idea how to bring anyone back to it. For one, people were dating with apps these days. That was something he completely missed out on. But now, he found himself single and lonely, and not sure what to do about it.

Maybe that's why Liz's message hit him so hard.

He had mostly forgotten about her. And even though he thought he was in love with her when he was 17, he wasn't sure if that's what it was now that he was an adult. She was always just a person that he obsessed about. She was the focus of most of his fantasies at the time, even though he didn't really know how tall she was.

He lathered shaving cream over his cheeks and chin. Was this the inner child work his therapist wanted him to do? Was he supposed to indulge the fantasies he created twenty years ago?

It didn't really matter if that's what his therapist meant or not. He was going to do just that.

The plan that evening was pretty standard. The class of 2001 was going to meet up at one of those janky chain restaurants by the mall to have dinner in one of the private banquet rooms. If you purchased a ticket to the reunion, you got two drink tickets. The attendance list was small, owing mostly to the fact that people who had access to Facebook often didn't feel like they needed to attend a reunion. After the dinner, they would head to the old high school gym and folks would mingle, maybe dance, and they would hand out awards and superlatives to folks based on how much people still looked like their senior photo or what they were doing now.

Brendan didn't think he would be included in any of that. While he wasn't a complete nerd back then, he wasn't popular either. In fact, he didn't stand out in any way that was worth mentioning. And that made him feel like he mostly didn't matter to those people.

That was why he didn't attend the ten-year reunion. But now that he was single and well, now that Liz wanted to meet up later that day, it seemed like fun.

He couldn't help but feel like meeting Liz this way was

meant to be. It was like he had to get divorced to make this all happen.

After the reunion, there had been talk of going out to the old bridge. That's where they'd get to meet up with their friends from the high school across town, just like they always used to. That's why Brendan had ultimately decided he would come. He wanted to see Liz, the elusive Liz he'd never gotten to meet. And everyone wanted to go see the old place one last time. The land was for sale and the rumor was that developers were all over it.

This was Brendan's last chance.

Twenty years ago, Cody had left the pack of students drinking around a portable radio and wandered away from the yard toward the trestle bridge that went over the river. The bridge was still sturdy enough, or so it looked, and Cody was drunk enough to try to walk across it.

The last thing anyone heard from Cody was a scream, and then a splash as his body hit the water.

Brendan had only ever had an art class with Cody, and he wasn't incredibly surprised when Cody died. Cody wasn't that smart. But he was drunk and popular and a daredevil that would do anything for attention.

As Brendan sat waiting by the railyard entrance for Liz to show up, Cody fell off the bridge, and the cops were called immediately from someone's brand new Nokia phone.

No one had been arrested as long as they promised to give a statement about what they saw and heard that night. And since everyone's stories matched up, it was a pretty cut and dry thing. Everyone stated that Cody wandered off, and then they could see him holding a flashlight as he tried to cross the bridge. Then, he screamed, and *splash*.

There was a little discrepancy about the scream. Some people said it was just a loud scream of distress. Others said it sounded like he screamed *who are you?* But no one could say for sure.

And it wasn't like anyone could ask Cody. He fell off the bridge, screamed, splashed, and his body wasn't found until a week later.

It took that long to drag the lake, and it churned up more old car parts and mud than anything else.

That was when the legend of the old railyard had a bit of a resurgence.

Brendan hadn't really remembered the origin of the legend, but it was something that people talked about in the city. There was a story about a woman in the great depression waiting for her true love to come back after he hopped a train. He told her he'd be back, but never came. Eventually, she killed herself in grief by jumping off the old trestle bridge. And when her body was found, they could tell she'd been pregnant.

The legend was that she haunted the old railyard, that you could see her glide over the bridge. But Brendan had gotten drunk there so many times growing up that it didn't seem possible for that story to be real. He'd never seen anything. And he definitely didn't see anything the night Cody died.

For some, it became a cautionary tale about the virtues of waiting until marriage. For the boys of the city, it became a great thing to tell their girlfriends to scare them into cuddling up a little closer as they sat at the railyard making out. For the historical society, it was an excuse to throw a special commemorative picnic near the railyard every year.

To Brendan, it didn't mean anything. He'd always heard it growing up. But he didn't care much for the story. And he didn't really believe in ghosts.

Brendan looked down at his phone again. He didn't know what he expected. He'd already exchanged information with everyone and RSVPed where he needed to. Did he expect Liz to message him again? They'd already firmed up the plan. They would meet at the railyard the way they meant to twenty years ago.

But he was anxious. What if it didn't happen *again*? What if Liz didn't like him? What if she thought he looked lame and old? What if she was married?

He really just wanted a message from her. Something that let him know she was just as excited as he was. She had to be, right?

He hoped so. He didn't know if he had that ability anymore—to make women nervous.

Brendan looked at the clothing options he brought. There was a shirt he really liked, and then there were three shirts that his ex-wife had bought for him and said they looked good. He had agreed with her, but they didn't feel like him. But did he want to feel like himself or did he want to look good?

He couldn't tell.

He picked up one of the shirts his ex-wife picked, a blue button down, and put it on. She was right about clothes most of the time, and he didn't want to look like an inept adult. He put on a pair of jeans and shoes that weren't quite nice so he didn't look like he was trying too hard, but also weren't bad either.

Before he left, he cleaned up the hotel room just in case Liz wanted to come back with him. He didn't know if she would, but he hoped. Surely she messaged him because she wanted to see him. He felt so out of practice. And he couldn't tell if he should keep the box of condoms in the suitcase, or not. The drawer of the nightstand was too close to the Bible, and that stressed Brendan out.

The divorce had given him more guilt and shame lately than he could handle, and he didn't need it now. He decided to keep the condoms in his suitcase and hope it wasn't awkward for him to go grab them if necessary.

He grabbed his phone out of his pocket again to see if Liz had messaged him. Maybe she was also nervous or stressed. He didn't know. But there was no message, and no status update or anything from her profile.

He put his phone back in his pocket and decided to head out. He'd go grab a beer at a nearby bar by himself first, and then head over to the restaurant. That would help him chill out a little and make it easier for him to be cool through the dinner. He hadn't been this nervous in a really long time.

———

BETTY LEE WAS A MOSTLY good girl. Or so she felt. Hadn't she gone to church every Sunday? Hadn't she prayed before bed? Hadn't she done her chores every day without complaining too much?

She was unequivocally good. Said "please" and "thank you" and dressed the way a good girl ought to dress. But it was boring. And Betty Lee was done.

She was so tired of waiting. Waiting on everything. It felt like her life would never start. She was stuck at home or working in her parent's store. She stocked the shelves and smiled and said 'hello' when the customers came in. She went to school and got good grades. But she was so tired of it all. She had big plans.

She wanted to be a movie star. Or a singer. Or the fancy wife of a rich man. She didn't really care. All she wanted was a life that was more exciting than the one she had. And she couldn't see how to do that.

The Great Depression had done a number on the city and her parents' business, but they were mostly okay. And then, there were rumors of war. It just felt like everything was happening around her and not to her. It felt like she would spend her life rationing because of the Depression or because of war, or because she would find herself married to some boring man with six kids and they'd have to ration because that was more kids than Betty Lee could understand how to care for.

But she didn't feel that way when she talked to James. He was different.

First and foremost, he wasn't from Franklin. He hopped a train at the railyard one day, and he made himself at home.

He was different and interesting and most importantly, he didn't think like everyone else in Franklin. And even though Betty Lee had spoken to him just once outside her parents' store, she felt something special about him. It could've been his black hair or his blue eyes, she didn't know. But she felt like he was perfect in every single way, and she knew she had to be with him.

Even if that meant hopping on a train and riding the rails with him.

But the problem was that she didn't know where to find him.

She'd tried to ask around after she met him, but that was a bad idea. Firstly, all the folks in Franklin tried to tell her to stay away from those men that ride the rails. And then secondly, they'd tell her daddy that she was looking around for those fellas. And that meant that Betty Lee was in trouble.

She'd been locked in a closet to say the holy rosary for three hours the first time. The next time, it was five hours and followed by a threat to send her to a convent.

So she changed her approach and kept her eyes open. She found herself walking around the city for various reasons—to deliver groceries to the older residents, to help out at church, or volunteer at events for the local city council.

Her parents were proud. All that praying and discipline did some good. And their daughter was becoming an upstanding member of the community. Maybe they could avoid the convent and she would be married after she graduated in a year.

But Betty Lee knew what she was doing. She was looking for him. She knew James hadn't left yet. She knew he was still in town, but didn't know where he was. Or where any of the other rail riders were for that matter. She was a nice girl and therefore didn't know what folks who weren't nice girls were up to.

But she kept an eye out, and then it happened. She saw him.

James walked into her parents' store on a Monday afternoon. Both her parents had gone home for the afternoon, and left Betty Lee to lock up. She'd been very bored and hot with the summer sun beating in through the window. She had been in a particular state of despair, thinking about how she was stuck in this boring town for the rest of her life and how she would never know excitement and adventure. She kept thinking that when she graduated, she'd marry one of the dull boys from school who would grow up and take over her parents' store. She hated that idea.

While she frowned and thought about where her life was headed, the door to the shop opened. She plastered a smile on her face and spoke.

"Good afternoon," she said, without turning to the customer.

He smiled. "Well, good afternoon to you too."

She spun quickly. "Hi. Um. Hi there."

"Well, hi there to you too." He leaned on the counter and smiled at her.

She blushed. "Can I help you?"

He looked her up and down, his blue eyes taking her in. "Maybe you can."

Betty Lee could feel the heat under her skin rise from her chest to her neck to her cheeks. He was perfect. Or at least, he seemed that way to her. She could forgive the dirty shirt and pants since his eyes were so blue. His smile was big, and there was some mischief behind it.

"I'm looking for a loaf of bread," he said.

Betty slumped a little. The one thing they didn't have. "I'm sorry," she said. "But we don't have any. We've got all the canned goods you could want," she offered. "Mrs. Washington runs a bakery down the street, though."

She couldn't help but feel sad to be sending him away after she finally found him again.

He seemed to weigh it over in his mind before speaking. "No. I don't think that will do." He smiled, his eyes gleaming a bit. "You know, I would much rather make a purchase here, and support this business." He winked.

She felt flustered. What did that mean? If she were a girl from a big exciting city, she would know. She would know what to say. She would even have said something witty and sophisticated at that point. But she wasn't. She was boring old Betty Lee from boring old Franklin. So she stood there in her parents' store and smiled awkwardly, not sure what to do next.

He finally spoke. "What time do you get off work?"

That was a good question. Betty had spent all afternoon daydreaming about leaving Franklin and falling in love and traveling in extravagant ways that she had no idea what time it was. She looked up at the clock on the wall.

"We close in five minutes," she said, her hands shaking a bit as she looked over the counter at him.

His grin widened. "That's perfect," he said. "Because I think you can help me."

"Absolutely!" She said, without thinking. She didn't even wait for him to explain what he needed.

———

BRENDAN WAS REALLY STARTING to regret that beer he had before meeting up with everyone. Or rather, those three beers.

He sat down at the bar and thought that he'd quickly down one and then call it a day. But that's not how it went. He kept looking at the Facebook event and going through the names of everyone who RSVPed to attend that night. There were so many people he hadn't even thought about in so many years. And all of them looked way better on paper than he did.

People he thought of as glue sniffing idiots back in the day now owned their own businesses. People that he felt were beneath him in the social hierarchy had not only gotten hot after graduation, but they'd started really pretty families that were still intact.

He kept scrolling through the group's notifications and clicking on profiles. He kept finding evidence that maybe he shouldn't go. He felt like maybe he should skip the reunion and go back to the hotel, maybe watch porn or something and then leave the next morning. He'd already paid for the room, so he wasn't going to just leave. But damn. He hadn't expected this.

So as he kept scrolling and clicking on notifications and searching through the photos his long-lost classmates had posted, he kept ordering beers, hoping they would quell the anxiety.

But they didn't.

And finally, when he realized how much he'd had, it was time to meet up at the restaurant across the street. He put a few mints in his mouth and hoped no one thought he was a lush.

The bartender winked at him as he left, and he thought that maybe if it all went tits up, he could just head back to this bar and at least flirt with her for a while. There was no way she was going to come back to the hotel room with him, and he wasn't out of the game so long that he thought he actually had a chance with a young blonde girl, but at least she made him feel nice while he scrolled through Facebook.

He crossed the street, feeling really awkward about showing up alone. Everyone else had a spouse or had met up with friends they'd stayed in touch with. But not him. He was awkwardly entering an Italian restaurant to meet up with people he hadn't seen in years.

At first, he made a beeline for the bar in the banquet room. It was pretty full, but he didn't recognize anyone. He grabbed a beer and stood in the corner of the room. Maybe he got there too early. There were posters and balloons hung up for the occasion, and several enlarged photos of big events their senior year—the football team taking state, the aftermath of the senior prank involving toothpaste and the principal's car, a big overhead shot taken from the top of the gym of the dancefloor at prom, and a photo from graduation of all the caps flying in the air.

And of course, there was the obligatory picture of Cody Dempsey, with a little memorial caption beneath it.

It was strange to Brendan that anyone really cared about those 4 years. He didn't remember most of it, though he'd always been told that it was the best time of his life. He used to think that his family was the best time of his life, but now, after the divorce, he tried to remain optimistic and assume that the best time was yet to come. And looking at those photos that lined the room helped him feel that way, especially since there wasn't a single photo of him.

Not that he expected there would be. He'd always been someone in the background, a supporting character.

Even in his marriage.

His wife called the shots. Hell, she had even told him when he needed to ask her to marry him. She decided which house they bought, when they would have kids, and she had even decided which promotions at work she wanted him to go for.

Overall, she had been very helpful to him. He wasn't always the sort of person to make stuff happen. But now, he could see why that had been a problem, and why he was still standing in the background of a party that he decided to attend on the off-chance he might get laid.

People continued to filter into the room, and he nodded

and smiled while holding his beer in his hand. Around the time he finished his first, he noticed someone making eyes at him.

He turned and smiled, not quite sure where to place her.

"Brendan?" She asked, tilting her head and smiling. Her blonde hair was piled in unruly curls on top of her head, and she was swaying back and forth in a pair of too-tall platform sandals that made her just barely come up to Brendan's chest.

That's when he realized who it was.

"Sarah?" Brendan asked, smiling.

She came to him and wrapped her arms around him in a hug. "It's so good to see you, partner!"

"Ha. Haven't had chem lab in a while, though. Are we still partners?"

"I think so! You can't break the bonds that are formed during a titration experiment."

Brendan hadn't thought much about Sarah in years. In fact, he didn't think much of her back then either. She had been his lab partner, a small, nerdy girl who was in all the dorkiest clubs. He vaguely remembered getting invited to one of her birthday parties, but he blew it off to hang out with his friends and get drunk.

She had always been so nice to him, but he had never been interested. Until now.

Or maybe he wasn't interested?

He didn't know. Honestly, he'd consumed a few beers and was just so ready to sleep with anyone who wasn't his ex-wife that it honestly didn't matter. And while she didn't look like a model, Sarah wasn't bad looking. He noticed she didn't have a ring on her left hand. Maybe she might be fun to hang out with tonight, he thought.

No, he reminded himself. He was going to meet Liz.

But if Liz didn't show, well. Sarah was a good backup plan.

"So, are you here with your wife?" She asked, smiling broadly.

If she knew he was married, she probably knew he had gotten a divorce. Facebook betrayed all. But Brendan was feeling warm and buzzed and thought it might be fun to just flirt. He could warm up with Sarah, and then later, he'd be ready for Liz.

"Single now, actually," he said, scratching the back of his head. "We had a good run, I guess."

He could see the slight twinkle in Sarah's eye.

"Oh, that's too bad. I'm so sorry to hear that," she said. "If it makes you feel any better, I'm here by myself too. I mean, I guess I'm single too." She blushed.

Brendan could believe it. Sarah had always been weird, at least to him. But he kept his opinions to himself.

"No way," he said. "That's hard to believe." Then, he switched the subject quickly. "So, what do you do?"

Brendan led the two of them to the bar and got himself another beer and some wine for her. She told him that she worked for some tech company doing something in marketing and that her job was basically to go live on social media and lead webinars to entice new customers to purchase their product. Brendan tried to pay attention and follow along, but it all sounded weird and he didn't really care that much.

He told her about his two kids, the work he did in the accounting department of a hospital, and how he had just gotten a pretty cool apartment in the city.

She hung on his every word.

People came and went. Brendan found himself having fun. Sarah was different. At least, not the type of woman that he usually enjoyed spending time with. She was smart and funny, and she made really topical jokes. Brendan couldn't help but feel a little inferior. He wondered if he'd feel the same way talking with Liz.

Brendan wondered what cheap and shitty restaurant Liz

was at, what drinks she was having, and if she was about to head over to the auditorium at East Franklin High while he made his way to West Franklin. The idea made him feel weird, like butterflies in his stomach, like he was finally getting close.

"So, see you there?" Sarah had interrupted his thoughts. She kept doing that.

"Yeah," he said, more briskly than he intended, noticing her reaction to it. "Yes," he said, more softly. "I'll definitely be there. Are you coming to the railyard later?" He asked, feeling cool for knowing about an after party.

Sarah's eyes widened. "They're doing a party out there?"

Brendan nodded. "Yeah. We're going to meet up with East Franklin people. It's going to be fun. I think someone is getting a keg."

Sarah looked down at her feet. "I never went out there when we were in school. I never got invited. But it might be fun to come."

Brendan smiled, taking her hand and looking into her eyes. "Yeah. It will be. We can talk more about it when we're in the auditorium."

———

BETTY LEE DIDN'T KNOW what she was doing, but she did know that butterflies were in her stomach something fierce. She wasn't one to walk around the town with a boy, especially since her parents were so strict and the town was so small and everyone would talk. But today, today she didn't mind it.

She could listen to James talk all day. His voice was happy and smooth, and he always knew just what to say. He talked about all the big cities he'd been to, like Chicago. That sounded really glamorous to Betty Lee. She wondered how she could get there, and if James would take her, and what a logical timeline for marriage for the two of them would be.

It didn't seem to register with her that he wasn't a good

date, nor was she able to think about the logical limitations of his lifestyle. Betty Lee wanted excitement and adventure, and James seemed to have that covered with riding the rails and all. But Betty Lee wasn't being realistic with herself. In all her best day dreams, excitement and adventure were tied up with money and fancy things. She was never train hopping. She was never waking up in a new town just because she could. She was always covered in the finest clothes and pearls and sitting next to the richest man in the room who kept pouring her more champagne.

That's what her idea of excitement and adventure had always been. But there was something about James that put that feeling in her stomach. It was the butterflies. He made her feel the same way she felt when she thought about being a movie star.

So she kept following him around town that day while he talked. She had offered to help him, but she still wasn't clear on what that help was, or where they were going.

Finally, as the sun set, they wound up on the banks of the river, just fifty or so yards from the trestle bridge. Before they sat down, James made a big show of putting down a handkerchief for her to sit on, so she wouldn't ruin her skirt.

Betty thought it was silly, but at the same time, she appreciated the gesture, and in her mind, it was proof that James was indeed a gentleman and maybe just down on his luck and later he'd come into some kind of inheritance and marry her up right and proper.

Betty Lee listened to James talk about all the places he'd been, and listened even more when he made a list of all the places he'd take her. When he finally made a confession of love while holding her hand, Betty Lee almost fainted from joy. As the moon rose up over the river, he leaned in slowly and kissed her, the first kiss that Betty Lee ever had.

It seemed slow and right and perfect and just like everything it was supposed to be. She didn't have anything to compare it to, but it was everything she'd ever hoped for. And as his hands moved from the back of her neck to her back, to her waist, to her thigh, she could hear a voice in her head saying *no*.

But that voice never spoke aloud.

She wasn't completely naïve. She knew where babies came from, mostly. There were enough farms in the small town that raised all manner of animals. So she'd seen firsthand how it was done. She'd asked around enough and knew what happened to girls who managed to have babies without getting married. She also knew that she didn't particularly care to have a baby. At least, not yet.

She couldn't imagine what a life of adventure looked like with a child, and she didn't want to wait until she lost the baby weight to get her fancy dresses.

But that didn't mean that everything didn't feel good. It was all new, and everywhere James put his hands was right. She knew she shouldn't. She knew if she got caught by her parents (who were probably wondering where the hell she was at that moment) she'd be in trouble. So much trouble. She'd be in the convent for sure.

But she didn't want to stop. As her heartbeat quickened, as James put his hands in places that Betty Lee didn't know she could be touched, she couldn't help but think this was the start of some grand adventure. This was it.

And later that night, as she was putting her clothes back on and walking back into town, having left James at the rail-yard, she couldn't help but feel adventurous. Surely nothing that felt like that could be bad. Surely this was just the first step in her life as an adventurous and worldly woman. Why, by this time next year, she'd be out of school and she and James could marry and they'd go to places like Chicago and maybe even New York City. Maybe by then he'd come into his inheritance. (She couldn't remember if he said he had one or if she'd made it all up.)

And maybe by then, her parents would see what a perfect gentleman he always was.

———

THE GYM still smelled like sweat and mildew, which meant that the roof was probably still leaking, and probably would be until the building was razed to the ground.

Brendan looked around, feeling grumpier than he had in a long time. He wasn't there for the reunion. He was there to see Liz, who was at her own reunion and who he wouldn't see until they made it out to the railyard.

There were more pictures hanging around the gym, and it made him realize how much he had missed out on. Had there always been that many clubs? Had there always been that many sports to play? Why didn't he know about it?

He started to suspect that spending his teen years clicking around on the nascent internet wasn't time well spent. Though, maybe it would be if Liz turned out to be what he hoped.

The music bumped from speakers hanging in the rafters, the noise crackling through the shoddy equipment. It was all songs from the late nineties and early two thousands, just the top forty radio stuff that he didn't care for then, and also didn't happen to care much for now. Groups of women belted out every word, dancing in a circle around their shoes and purses.

Good for them, he thought, trying to figure out who was who so he could mentally congratulate himself for not getting fat like the former popular girls did.

He had posted up on the bleachers, holding a can of cheap beer in his hand. That's what they were serving, canned beer and boxed wine. It was all set up on a table in the back of the room, and there were a few snacks too. But mostly, it wasn't anything special and Brendan wanted to know why tickets to the reunion were so expensive if it was going to be like this.

After a while, Sarah found him and asked him to dance. He said yes, even though he felt self-conscious. She wasn't bad looking, after all, and it would be good for people to see him with a woman, right? No one would ask about the divorce if he was too busy leaning on Sarah.

They twirled through a couple of songs, and Brendan could feel a drunk coming on. He'd officially had too much, but he didn't care, not really. It was supposed to be a party, after all. And it wasn't like he had the kids that weekend. He had a badass hotel room, and he could do whatever he wanted with it.

Momentarily, he thought about taking Sarah back there right then. He'd been looking down her dress for the past couple of dances, not in a pervy way. But it was there and he could look nonchalantly enough, so why not? She had a nice body, even if she didn't have a face like Liz. And he was single. She was single. They were both drinking. Why not?

But then he remembered what he was really there for. Liz.

Was she even going to show up?

He didn't know, and wouldn't know until he got to the rail-yard. But even if she didn't, Sarah was going to the railyard too, and well. She'd been hanging on him all night, right? She wanted him. She had to.

He smiled at Sarah as she looked up at him. Brendan knew he was getting laid no matter what. And to him, in that moment, that was an absolute win.

The music quieted down and *Glycerine* by Bush came on. The DJ, or at least, the person manning the playlist, called for a remembrance dance for Cody Dempsey. Some of the women who were still circled up and dancing started to cry as they leaned on their friends.

"Did you know him?" Sarah asked, slowing down and putting her head on Brendan's chest.

"Not really, no. I mean, we had one class together. But it wasn't like we were friends or anything."

"Same," Sarah said, pausing for a moment. "Do you think he's out there?"

"On the dance floor?" Brendan asked, worried that perhaps he was starting to sound drunk.

Sarah laughed. "No, silly. At the railyard. Do you believe in ghosts?"

Then it was Brendan's turn to laugh. "Nope. Not at all."

Sarah nodded slowly. "Yeah. I don't know. I never went out to the railyard growing up because I was never invited, but I was pretty happy to not be invited, just because it meant that I would never run into that ghost. And then when Cody Dempsey died the way he did, so many people believed that it was the ghost."

Brendan racked his brain. Ghost? He could vaguely remember the urban legend. "I never saw a ghost out there."

"But what about Cody? Do you think the ghost dragged him down to the river with her?"

Brendan leaned in to whisper in Sarah's ear. "I think Cody was so drunk that he couldn't walk straight, and that's why he fell off the bridge."

"Did you party like that?" Sarah seemed to be judging him.

Brendan shook his head and hoped that he didn't look drunk while he did it. "Not until college when we were in our dorm. Back then, I was too busy trying to look cool. It didn't work out for me. I quietly sipped my drink and faded into the background."

Sarah put her hand around his waist like a hug while they danced. "I'm glad you came here. I didn't know if I was going to see anyone I knew, and well. I'm glad I got to see you."

Brendan put his arm around her too, holding her just a little closer as *Glycerine* played.

———

BETTY LEE KNEW something was wrong.

Firstly, she felt like shit. She was tired all the damn time. The most minor of smells made her vomit. And though she had been able to set her watch to her period since she was 13, it was late.

She wasn't stupid. She knew what was going on. But she didn't want to say it out loud. And hadn't her aunt had a few miscarriages? Maybe she would get lucky.

It wasn't that she didn't want a baby, at least, not exactly. But there was so much to do, so many adventures to have. And well. This baby really would put a damper on things. In all her dreams of walking through Chicago, she never had a baby on her hip. It was always a fur stole around her neck.

And then, there was the matter of James. Where was he?

She hadn't seen him since that night, and she had asked around with a few of the other rail riders to find that he had up and gone.

That didn't seem right.

Wasn't he a good man? Wasn't he going to take her on adventures? Weren't they destined to be together? Doubly so since she was now pregnant with his child?

She knew she had some time until she was showing, and if she could find him and let him know what happened, well, surely he'd do the right thing. He had to, right? That's what men did.

She kept telling herself that, but it didn't seem to matter. There was still a part of her that didn't believe it. She had to stay strong.

James would be back soon. Of course he would.

———

AFTER *GLYCERINE,* Brendan was ready to ask Sarah back to his hotel at that moment. But the trance was broken when the song transitioned to *Back that Thing Up*, and all the women on the dance floor eagerly looked for men to grind on.

All in all, it reminded Brendan a lot of senior prom. It was a weird environment, and he was surrounded by folks he didn't really know, and was more eager for what would happen after the dance than anything else.

"Oh my God! It's Jenna Swanson!" Sarah pointed across the gym. "Let's go say hi to her!"

Brendan looked across the gym at a woman he didn't know or remember. "Go ahead. I'll meet back up with you. I'm going to run to the bathroom."

"Okay, cool. Just come find me," she said, smiling at him with her hand on his arm. "Don't leave me too long. Jenna can talk and I'm not super interested in her trying to recruit me for whatever multilevel marketing company she works for currently."

Brendan smiled. "I'll swoop in at the right time, I promise."

He watched as Sarah walked away, wondering why he had never noticed what a nice ass she had before. The idea of Liz was getting less and less appealing. Did he really want to go to the railyard?

He exited the gym and went to the bathroom at the end of the hall. It also still smelled and looked the same after all those years.

He took his time in the bathroom, checking his phone and fixing his hair.

Did he like Sarah? He thought so. But they hadn't talked about a lot. Or at least, not the important stuff.

Wasn't that why he used to like Liz? He felt like they chatted online about big things. Like the questions he could stay up all night pondering. But that was twenty years ago. And he hadn't had a conversation like that with her in a long time, nor did he really have those conversations anymore. It wasn't because he didn't want to, it was more that he just didn't really have the time or energy for them. He was an adult, and staying up all night chatting on the internet was not something he was interested in.

But almost as if on cue, she messaged him.

"Can't wait to finally meet you. Kind of feel like it's all meant to be."

Brendan splashed some water on his face, hoping to wake up a little. All of this was so new and different, and it had been so long since he'd been dating. But now, there were two women that wanted to hang out with him. What was he going to do with that?

He knew he needed to keep being nice to Sarah. It may be leading her on, but being a dick and pushing her away wasn't an option either. So he would go back to the gym and dance with her, and when the night ended at around 11, they would all go together to the railyard. He'd probably need a ride. That would be fine. Sarah could take him, and then after she spent the night with him, she could take him to get his car.

That was, if he spent the night with Sarah. Wasn't he going to try to spend the night with Liz?

This was way out of his comfort zone, and he wasn't sure he could make it all work. But he left the bathroom and went back to the gym just in time to rescue Sarah from Jenna's sale's pitch.

BETTY WAS DESPERATE.

She needed a place to stay. Her family had found out. Hell. They probably knew all along. It had been decided that she'd go to a special hospital run by nuns to give birth, and the baby would be put up for adoption immediately. Then, Betty would stay there and work at the hospital with the nuns for the rest of her life.

At least, that's what her family had decided. They were done with her, and didn't want a daughter that brought them shame and embarrassment representing them in their store.

The only issue was that Betty felt she should be consulted in all of this. She didn't exactly love the idea of having a child, but it was hers, and she was damned if she wasn't going to keep it. And there was absolutely no way in hell that she was going to work at a hospital with a bunch of nuns for the rest of her life. She didn't want that, and couldn't see any adventure in it.

So, she made a plan. It wasn't much of a plan.

She ran away.

And after she left, she ran out of plan. She found herself sitting in the hay loft of a barn on the edge of town, just waiting for the sun to set so she could get back on the road and make her way somewhere. There had to be a place. Someone needed a good worker or she could live in barns and steal food from nearby farms when she needed.

It wasn't ideal, but it sounded better than what her parents had planned for her.

As she sat in the hay loft, she rested her hand on her belly. It wasn't big yet, and she was probably only four months or so along. But she smiled as she thought about who her child would be. If it were a boy, she'd absolutely name it after his father. Even though he wasn't there now, she held out hope that James would find her. Wasn't that the sort of grand gesture that romance was made of? He would seek her out, so distraught that he'd left her in such a state. And maybe by then he would've come into his inheritance and they could have a quiet little home to raise their son.

Unless it was a daughter. And then, Betty Lee thought it was only fitting to name it after her. She'd never much cared for Elizabeth, but she did like all the variations. Her daughter could be an Eliza, or maybe a Liz. Betsy was fun too. But it made sense to name the babies after their parents, and well. Even if this baby didn't have a very traditional start in this world, Betty Lee would make damn sure that the baby had a good upbringing anyway.

No one would know about how Betty Lee left home, or how and when the baby was conceived. They didn't need a fancy wedding. They'd go to the court house as soon as James found her. And then they'd raise their baby as if it was the most natural thing in the world. She'd tell folks that she was an orphan, and they'd live the rest of their lives outside of Franklin and with the family they made themselves.

She kept going over the details, making sure they stuck. That was how Betty Lee lived. If she kept daydreaming enough, it would come true. Hadn't she always dreamed of adventure? And what was she up to now?

It wasn't exactly the adventure she pictured, but there weren't that many ways to get out of Franklin. And well, she was always the type to do stuff her own way, even if it made it a lot harder in the long run.

But she knew if she kept thinking about the lovely house they'd buy together, James would feel it. He would know that she loved him and that she was carrying his baby, and that he needed to come find her.

So as she sat in that hay loft ignoring how hungry she'd become and how tired she was and how much her feet hurt and how she'd love to sit in a nice soft chair, she thought about all the ways her story could go.

Maybe they'd buy a farm in Minnesota. It wasn't her favorite idea, but it was a good way to raise children, and she'd be the type of parent to make sure her children were more worldly, so they'd visit museums and theaters on the weekends. That did sound nice, a little city and country wrapped up in one life.

Or maybe they'd live in a fancy apartment in a city, and

they'd take the elevator every morning when they went down-stairs to start their day. That sounded fun and like a life Betty Lee could enjoy.

Maybe they'd live in a fancy hotel in New York City, while James did very important work with his inheritance. She tried to fill in the details of that dream, but Betty Lee didn't know anything about New York City, and she definitely didn't know anything about what folks did with large sums of money in the city. Maybe he would start a business, but the more she thought about this dream, the more she pushed it out of her head. She couldn't piece it all together and it was full of holes.

Like this plan, she thought.

But she wasn't going to give up. It was running away, or giving up her baby. And she wasn't a coward. She could do this. She got herself into this mess with James, and she could get herself out of it with him.

A few tears rolled down her cheek as the sun set. She could see the light dwindling as it shined between the slats in the barn. The family that owned the farm had gone mostly quiet, and she had heard them all walk up to the house earlier anyhow. Now the only sound she heard were mice rustling in the hay, and the mean old barn cats pouncing.

It was time to go. She had to keep moving if she was going to get away.

———

"THAT WAS SO CLOSE," Sarah said, wrapping Brendan in a hug as Jenna left the two of them for better prey. "She really wanted me in her downline."

"I don't know what that means," Brendan said, shrugging. "Sounds dirty…"

"Yeah, you're a guy. Your friendships haven't been tainted by the hustle culture of multilevel marketing companies. I swear sociologists will look back on this time and analyze how these corrupt companies destroyed women's ability to connect with one another while promising to empower them to work together."

Brendan still didn't get it, but he loved how smart Sarah sounded, and that when she spoke, she included him in the conversation like she thought he was as smart as her. He knew he wasn't, but at the end of the day, it didn't really matter. If she thought it, it was good enough for him.

Would Liz think the same way?

The party continued as the music died down and some of the student council reps from twenty years ago took the stage.

"Seems like such a long commitment," Brendan said. "You run for student council in high school because it looks good on your college application, and you're stuck with reunion duty for the rest of your life."

Sarah laughed and shushed him.

He liked that. It had been a really long time since he made a woman laugh. He put his arm around her, not in a possessive gesture, but in a comforting and friendly one, as if to say that he liked her.

As the student council representatives talked, Sarah put her arm around Brendan's waist, and they listened as people were called to the stage. One of their classmates opened a successful business and received some sort of cheap looking trophy for it. Another had become a politician and was recognized for that. One woman who Brendan remembered from some of his classes received a cheap plastic trophy for becoming a published author, but Brendan always thought she was so stuck up that he didn't even clap for her.

The awards continued and neither Brendan or Sarah were recognized for anything, which was just as well. Brendan didn't really mind not having to pay attention, and he liked getting to stand next to Sarah, especially if she was going to hold onto him too.

After the awards were passed out, the student council president, Amy Walsh, took the stage. Some people clapped and cheered before she even spoke.

Amy smiled and waited for everyone to quiet down.

Brendan giggled at her outfit—a hot pink tulle skirt and a black tank top. "What is she wearing?" He whispered to Sarah, who covered her mouth in a fit of giggles.

"As many of you know," Amy began, "on the night we graduated, Cody Dempsey died at the railyard. I know there are plans to head there tonight so that we can see our friends from East Franklin, but I want to caution everyone to be very, very careful. It's been twenty years, and it's not like the bridge or the railyard were in good working order when we partied back in the day. So know this, if you choose to attend the after party at the railyard, you are doing so of your own volition, and West Franklin High and the student council representatives responsible for this reunion are in no way liable for your actions."

She paused, looking across the crowd.

"With that, I wanted to take a moment to remember Cody. He was a good guy, a star athlete, homecoming king, and my boyfriend. We had plans to attend the same university, and we had even talked about marriage."

Brendan couldn't tell if she was being honest or if she was playing it up, but she brushed a small tear from her cheek.

"He was the best first boyfriend a girl could have."

"I doubt that," Brendan muttered. "He was dumber than a bag of hammers."

Sarah poked him in the ribs to be quiet, but a person in front of him that he didn't recognize turned around and snickered in agreement.

"So, with that, I wanted to share this video tribute I made for Cody. Cody, baby, I wish you were here."

The DJ hit play and *"One Sweet Day"* started playing through the speakers. Behind Amy, a video slideshow was projected onto the wall. The photos were old and grainy, originally taken on film and digitized for this purpose.

There were photos of Cody on the field, some newspaper clippings, a few photos from before school dances, and then there were the candid shots that had probably been taken by disposable cameras at house parties. All in all, it was nice, but it was so odd that they spent so much time memorializing this man.

Or, at least Brendan thought it was.

Now they were more than twice the age that Cody had been when he died. Surely everyone could see that he was just a dumb kid that partied too much.

As if she felt the same way, Sarah stood up on her toes to whisper in Brendan's ear.

"This is so morbid," she said.

Brendan nodded, wishing she would spend the rest of the video just whispering in his ear. It didn't matter what she said.

He took a deep breath and remembered that he may be meeting Liz that night, and immediately felt guilty for having his arm around Sarah. But not guilty enough to move it.

He didn't know how he was going to handle this, but he did know that he needed to chill out and stop fantasizing about which girl would be in bed with him in his hotel room until he knew for sure.

———

BETTY WOKE up in the bedroom she grew up in.

She couldn't remember exactly how she got there, but she knew that she tried to walk to the next city, and she just passed out. She used to be able to go without eating for a long time, but now, well. She got dizzy the minute the baby got hungry. So, she had passed out on the side of the road. And she vaguely remembered her parents coming to get her after someone had found her. And she knew they picked her up into their truck and brought her home.

And that's where she was that morning.

Tears streamed down her cheeks. She could hear her parents rustling around downstairs. She could smell something cooking. She was so hungry. She had no idea what she was going to do now.

She put her hands on her belly under the covers. She didn't want to think about a life without this baby. Even though she knew she was in no place to care for it. Even though she knew her parents hated her for it. Even though she was starting to think she may never see James again. She wanted this baby.

She could hear footsteps coming up the stairs. Betty Lee sat up.

Her mother walked in, her face stern and sallow like always. She brought a plate of eggs and toast to Betty and set them on the table by the bed. She looked down at her daughter, her hands clasped in front of her against her brown dress.

"You are causing a lot of trouble, you know."

Betty didn't say anything.

"You're lucky that Mr. Pritchard found you when he did. You could've been run over by some truck in the dark that didn't see you."

Betty kept staring.

"And now, Mr. Pritchard knows our daughter tried to run away. So, even though we tried to give you an opportunity to not embarrass us, you still did so."

Betty scowled.

"I know that you don't want to work at the hospital for the rest of your life, but you made your choice, Betty Lee. We all make choices every single day. And you made yours and now it's time to spend the rest of your life reflecting on it."

"And what if I want something else? I can go anywhere. You don't have to take me to the hospital. Instead of driving me there, drop me off anywhere, and you'll never hear from me again, I swear. Just take me anywhere. Leave me at a boarding house. Take me to the railyard and I'll hop a train. I will go anywhere. Just don't make me go there."

"This is very silly," her mother said in disgust. "You must stop acting like a child. You're no longer innocent anyway. You're going to the hospital. On Sunday, your father and I will skip church and drive you there. That's final."

Her mother turned around to leave. Not a single hair on her head swayed with her movement, and Betty Lee wondered how that woman always walked as if her spine were made of granite.

It didn't really matter though. Betty picked up the plate of food and finished it in less than a minute. She had two days to figure something out. And she knew her imagination was what got her into trouble that day. Maybe if she used it to think of an escape plan and less of using it as a way to wear fancy clothes, she'd be able to get out.

———

BRENDAN PULLED up to the railyard. Sarah had ridden along with him. They listened to some throwback Spotify station on her phone, and Sarah shared some bands that she used to listen to, none of which were played at the reunion.

Had Sarah always been this cool? He didn't know. He didn't pay much attention to her back in the day. She wasn't exactly uncool. She just wasn't fetish worthy, like Liz.

But that made Brendan wonder if he liked the idea of Liz more than he would actually like Liz. He didn't know, and he hoped that very soon this whole evening of wondering who he would go home with would be solved.

They got out of the car and Sarah looked around.

"So this is it, eh?"

Brendan nodded. "Yeah. It's not much. It's not great. But

it was what we had at the time. And no one ever got in trouble for getting wasted out here until the night that Cody died."

"I just always assumed it was cooler."

"Well, it was. When we were 17. We didn't really have great taste back then."

Sarah laughed. "It's really rustic," she said, scraping her strappy platform sandal through the dirt.

"Yeah," Brendan looked at her foot and then back at his car. "Hang on." He walked around the trunk and pulled out a blanket he used to sit on at his kids' soccer games.

They made their way to where the crowd of people were gathered. There was a keg and red Solo cups. There was also a Gatorade cooler full of something else. Brendan felt like they were all taking this opportunity to drink just like they did when they were younger.

He laid out the blanket for Sarah and then grabbed two beers. It didn't look like anyone from East Franklin was there yet. And he didn't know how he felt about being seen by Liz with Sarah, but he also felt like he wanted to spend the night with Sarah. And maybe more. She was funny and fun and cute and how he had not tried to date her in high school was blowing his mind.

They watched as their former classmates got drunker and drunker. Sarah leaned against him.

"You know," she said. "I had a crush on you in high school."

"You did?" Brendan asked, though he had suspected all along.

"Yeah. I wanted to ask you to so many things. But I didn't. I was scared. And you always seemed so cool so it was hard."

"You thought I was cool?" He made a shocked expression. "I think you may be the first."

Sarah laughed and looked down at her lap. "You were, though. You were smart and you got to hang out with everyone and you were always so secure in whatever you were doing. I loved it."

"Oh, damn. I think I pulled the wool over your eyes there. I pretended to be secure, but I mostly didn't do anything but spend my time alone at home or just chatting online. Remember chat rooms? I spent a lot of time doing that. Or just homework, or watching TV. I was mostly concerned with not being a nerd, so I did whatever I felt made me look chill. And it meant that I didn't do much."

"I didn't know that. You always seemed like you were above it all."

Brendan shrugged. "I don't think I was. I think I wished I was. But I always liked chemistry class with you. You are the only reason I made an A in that class."

It was dark, and the only light in the railyard came from the moon and some headlights, but Brendan could see that Sarah was blushing.

"So, do you live around here now?" Brendan asked, changing the subject and hoping he could make staying in his hotel room something that Sarah seemed to think she decided for herself, and not something that he brought up.

She nodded. "About an hour away. My mom is still in Franklin, but I live in Northaven. It's where I work."

————

BETTY LEE COULD FEEL the bottom of her feet bleeding, but she didn't have any other choice. She had to sneak out of the house that night, or it would be too late and she'd wind up at the hospital. She didn't think she'd be able to sneak away from there. They probably had all sorts of measures in place to make sure girls like her stayed put.

So she left the house barefoot so her parents wouldn't hear, and she forgot to bring her shoes. She'd been so absentminded since she got pregnant. She felt like she couldn't keep the days straight, she couldn't hatch a plan, and she was forgetting everything she needed to survive. But it was going to be okay, she told herself.

She made her way barefoot through the town, the dirt roads caking mud on her already bloody feet. She could walk through that town with her eyes closed, that's how well she knew it. And she couldn't wait to never think about Franklin again. She was going to get out, and she was going to do it the same way that James did.

The railyard wasn't far, but if she got there, she could get on an early train and then her parents would be so far behind her that they'd never find her. They'd probably figure out what she did, but if she was gone and not embarrassing them anymore, it was likely that her parents wouldn't come after her.

Afterall, they just wanted a quiet and upstanding life. And if she was gone, they had that.

She felt a tear run down her cheek. She still didn't feel like she was wrong for wanting to keep her baby. Or that she was wrong for what she did. Hadn't she had fun that day?

She did. And well, so what if it wasn't going to be a perfect adventure and who cared if she didn't have fancy movie star clothes? There wasn't anything to be done about it now. And even if she never saw James again, it wasn't like she was going to be alone with this baby forever.

She'd tell folks she was an orphan, and the baby's father had died too. That was simple enough, and honestly, who was going to question? Surely there would be someone that would take her in. Maybe she'd even fall in love again.

She didn't want to think about that. She didn't like how easily she had fallen in the first place, and she was starting to see why there were all those cautionary tales that warned girls not to do exactly what she had done.

But she couldn't think about that now.

As she made her way down Main Street, she stopped in

front of her parents' store. She had loved that place when she was a kid. It was the perfect place to go and play. She could wander up and down the shelves and pretend like she was a princess trapped in a maze just waiting for Prince Charming to save her. Or she could bring her dolls and let them play in the backroom and imagine what it would be like when she was a grown adult and had her perfect dream life.

But somewhere along the way, the store wasn't fun anymore. As Betty Lee looked in the windows of the building, she couldn't see any of the old magic. It was dingy and dusty, just like everything else in that small town. And it had the most mundane things. Flour and lard. Lye soap. Candy. The basic things that all stores sold.

And the longer that Betty Lee was stuck there, the more that store just became a prison. Her imagination had kept her dreaming of adventures, but she could no longer go on those adventures just by looking at the shelves. She had to imagine Hollywood or Chicago or New York City. She had to think about everywhere else.

The thought occurred to her that maybe she was destined to be stuck in this town for the rest of her life. That was what her parents had wanted. But the minute she didn't follow their little plan, she was going to be shipped right off.

Betty Lee couldn't have that. She looked around for something to throw through the window of the store—a last rebellious act against her folks. But she couldn't find anything, and at the end of the day, she didn't want to draw more attention to herself. She knew that it was a long time before the town woke up and headed to church, but she didn't need to give anyone a reason to wake up early.

She turned her back on the store and kept heading to the railyard. There was a train that left at 6:15. She had to get there.

———

SOMEONE WAS SHOOTING FIREWORKS, and Brendan definitely smelled weed. It was like all his former classmates were trying to live their best life from twenty years ago.

He could also tell that Sarah was getting nervous. She was trying to be cool, but at the same time, all the noise and debauchery wasn't a good look, and no one wanted to get arrested.

"Should we go?" He asked, hoping that she'd say no. He still wanted to see if Liz would show. There were a few East Franklin attendees already present, so he assumed it would only be a matter of time.

"No, that's fine," she said, smiling. "It's just a lot. Do they always drink like this?"

Brendan shrugged. "They did in high school. I have to say that I'm not sure why they're drinking this way now."

Sarah sipped her beer.

"So, are you staying in town for the night?" Brendan asked, but worried he sounded too eager. "I only ask because I'd hate for you to have to drive the hour back to Northaven when you've been drinking and it's so late. You know the cops are probably setting up checkpoints tonight because of the reunions."

Sarah shook her head. "I had talked with Kate Miller and Jessica Thorn about that. We were going to get a big suite and then take the weekend to get like mani-pedis and stuff and just be fancy. But then, the plan fell through, or someone didn't reserve in time, and then both of them ended up not coming. So yeah, I guess I am driving home tonight."

Brendan didn't want to extend the formal invitation. At least, not right then. He didn't want to lose his chance with Liz if there was a chance. But he kept that info in the back of his mind, just in case.

He couldn't tell if he was being slimy or not. But he also didn't think it mattered. Didn't people come to this sort of thing just to hook up with people they used to have crushes

on? That's what he wanted to do with Liz, and that's what
Sarah wanted to do with him. Everyone was playing a game,
he told himself. It wasn't like she would actually be upset if he
went home with Liz. Sarah was just shooting her shot, and
maybe she'd wind up with him that night. But maybe he'd
wind up with Liz. It didn't really matter to him at this point
who it was, just because he knew he was going to be sleeping
with someone either way.

And he hoped his ex-wife would find out about it. Like
maybe Liz or Sarah would tag him in a photo on Facebook.
He made a mental note to take whoever it wound up being
out to breakfast the next morning, then they could have a nice
photo taken together as they sipped coffee in clothes they
clearly wore the night before.

It was a good plan.

An engine revved somewhere behind them, and it seemed
like more and more people were arriving.

"Did you know anyone from East Franklin?" Brendan
asked.

Sarah shrugged. "One of my cousins went there for a time
before he got expelled. But I don't think he's going to the
reunion."

Brendan laughed. "I didn't really know anyone from there
either. But let's let them all filter in, and then after this drink,
maybe we can go."

Sarah smiled.

———

SHE HAD MISSED THE TRAIN.

Or it had left early.

Or maybe she was running behind.

Her feet hurt so much and she was so tired and stressed
out that she wasn't sure. Also, she didn't have a watch on her.
But she could see that the sun had already started to rise and

she knew that she had missed it. She couldn't tell by how much.

She walked toward the little station house where an occasional foreman worked, but it was empty that early on Sunday morning. There was no schedule posted anywhere either. She had to think. And she had to think good. She was so tired of not knowing what her next move should be, and she didn't know where else she could go.

She sat on the edge of the boarding platform, small as it was for the tiny Franklin railyard, and thought.

She had no one she could turn to at this point. She'd run away a second time, and if her parents caught her, she was off to the hospital with the nuns. And she had no idea where James was. She could ask a friend of hers, but that was not the best idea. For one, if she asked a friend, there was a chance they'd shun her because she'd gotten herself pregnant. And even if they didn't, the friend could only do so much before their parents started to ask questions.

That was the problem with Franklin. It was too small and no one had the sort of money or resources that the rich folks in movies had. She couldn't run to a rich friend and ask for a loan or a ride out of town. No one could offer her that. So she knew that she had to keep going on her own.

She couldn't say how long she sat there, but the sun came up further and started beating down on her. She could see how dirty and bloody her feet were then, with little bits of gravel stuck in her flesh. But she didn't care. Everything hurt —her feet, her back, her hips, her head, and her heart.

Betty Lee always considered herself to be too smart to despair. Her imagination and optimism were just too good. And if she were the type to despair, she wouldn't have made it so long living in Franklin.

But now, she didn't think she could keep her optimism going. There were no more options. There were no places to go. No one to help. And as she turned away from the railyard toward the center of town, she could see people out and about heading to church.

She had run out of time and options.

———

THE EAST FRANKLIN students slowly filtered in, and Sarah had agreed to one more beer. Brendan couldn't tell if she was having a good time, but she didn't argue when he floated the idea of another drink before they headed out.

He also still hadn't asked her if she wanted to come back to his hotel with him. He didn't really know how to ask without being a jerk. Would she say yes? And if she did, did it mean she wanted to sleep with him?

Generally, he understood that women and men tended to want the same thing, but also, it wasn't always on the same timeline, and he didn't know how she would feel about being propositioned by him.

Was that what he was doing, propositioning? He wasn't sure.

He had watched as hordes of people had entered the rail-yard, but there was no Liz. And since there was only one way to enter since the river was on the other side, he assumed she wasn't going to show.

Part of him felt relieved. He didn't know who Liz was, really. At least, not since high school. And even then, they'd only chatted online.

But now, he had a clear direction. And well, it was getting late and he could tell that Sarah wanted to leave. But he didn't want her to leave by herself.

"I have a question," Brendan said, downing the last of the foamy beer in the cup. "And I don't want you to think I'm a creep or anything."

Sarah sipped the last of her beer.

"I know that we just caught up with each other today and

all. But would you…" He trailed off and took a deep breath before speaking again much faster than he had the first time. "Would you be interested in coming back to my hotel? You don't have to and we can just grab drinks at the hotel bar where it's quiet if you'd like--"

"Yes." Her answer came quickly.

"Really?" He didn't mean to sound so shocked or excited.

"Yeah. I mean. I'd love to. It would be great to sit at the bar and chat or like, I don't know. Do whatever."

Brendan couldn't be sure, but it felt like the "do whatever" was very loaded with possibilities. He liked that.

"But," Sarah said, looking toward the keg. "We do have to stay for one more drink."

Brendan followed her gaze. Jason McKenzie was doing a keg stand, or trying to.

"I hate that fucking guy," Sarah said, finishing her beer. "He used to try to cheat off my tests in history class, and I would always give him the wrong answers and he was too dumb to figure it out."

Brendan laughed at that. "Seriously?"

"Yeah. He was just an asshole all the time. His mom was friends with my mom, so we grew up together, but then he got really popular and played all the sports, and well. He thought I'd just help him cheat because our moms were friends. But he was such an asshole to me."

Brendan looked on as Jason tried in vain to kick his legs up and hold himself up with his arms. But the years between graduation and the present had not been kind to him, and Jason was absolutely no longer the athlete he once was.

After Jason fell for the final time and took a little too long to get up, Brendan grabbed Sarah's cup and said, "Okay. Final drink. I'll grab it now."

"Maybe only half full," Sarah said, smiling.

Brendan nodded. As he stood, a person approached them.

"Sarah? Oh my god, you guys. It's Sarah!"

Then, a gang of women walked up to the blanket.

They all began speaking excitedly with one another, and Brendan could tell that these were Sarah's friends. But he couldn't say with certainty what any of their names were. He nodded toward the keg and made a gesture with his hands as if to say he'd be right back. Sarah nodded and continued talking with the group of women.

Jason McKenzie still laid on the ground, laughing at his circumstances. His friends sat back a few feet away in folding chairs, seeming to laugh at him, and not with him.

Brendan got in line at the keg, and looked around. When he felt his phone vibrate in his pocket, he pulled it out and checked it. A message from Liz.

"Over by the trestle bridge."

What the fuck? She had some of the worst timing and always had. Brendan couldn't tell whether he was glad she actually showed, or if he was pissed off that he'd already asked Sarah to go with him.

Well, he was going back to the hotel with Sarah no matter what. He'd decided at that moment. He couldn't handle being strung along by Liz anymore. And what the hell was she doing out by the bridge? No one was hanging out over there. The whole party was happening in the railyard. And she was just off by the river?

It didn't make sense. Unless she wanted to be alone with him…

Brendan chose not to respond. But curiosity was getting the better of him. Surely he could sneak a look at her, couldn't he?

He looked over his shoulder at Sarah, laughing with a group of women and chatting. The line for the keg was incredibly long given that Jason McKenzie had held it up for so long. No one would notice if he popped over to the bridge for a minute. He'd jog over there, get a look at Liz, and then jog right back.

No one would be the wiser. And then after he was done, he'd be back in line, get the beers, and then be off with Sarah where they would have a good conversation at the hotel bar, or, he hoped, where they would be naked in his hotel room.

———

THERE WASN'T much in the way of choices, and Betty Lee knew there were no more trains that day. She was out of luck. But, she thought, a railroad was just a road to a new station, and if she got on the good foot, she could make her way down the tracks and she'd eventually end up at the next station where she could actually hop a train without anyone from town seeing her, and she'd be on her way.

She'd be away from her parents and away from the nuns, and on her own living her adventure and giving herself some time to figure things out.

The town was bustling behind her, and she could hear the church bells start to ring and car engines rumbling down the road. This was the only way out.

So, with her feet still bloody, she started down the tracks until she got to the trestle bridge. She stood at the edge of it for a bit, wondering if she was brave enough to cross. Her balance had never been anything special, but now that she was pregnant, it was terrible. There were so many opportunities to fall, but she could cross slowly. No one was at the train yard. No one would see her. And by the time she was on the other side, everyone would be looking on the other side of town, probably assuming she'd hitched her way out on a farm truck or something.

She put her hands on her belly and said a quick prayer. She hadn't prayed much lately and she didn't know if God still listened to her or cared about her, but she did it anyway. It was a quick and silent wish for a safe crossing and a new life for her and her baby.

Then, she took the first step, slowly letting her feet come into contact with the ties of the bridge.

———

OUTSIDE THE CIRCLE of the party, the railyard was too dark. Brendan thought about texting Liz to get her to come back toward the party so he could see her, but then he didn't really want to respond to her since he planned to just leave with Sarah in a bit anyhow. So, he kept making his way toward the bridge.

He'd dropped the plastic cups somewhere, and stuck mostly to the shadows that clung around the trees that grew up around the old, unused tracks.

When he came to the bridge, he looked around. There was no one there.

It occurred to him for the first time that maybe he was being catfished. That hadn't really been a term in his vocabulary back then, when he first started talking with Liz. But now, it seemed obvious. And it would make sense that someone from high school would mess with him. He momentarily paled at the thought that there were probably some people making fun of him back in the day for believing that Liz was a real woman who wanted to meet up with him.

And now, well. Now it was just sad.

He had a really nice, really pretty girl waiting for him. Hell, she wanted to go back to a hotel with him. What the fuck was he doing? Was he really going to potentially mess up his evening to hang with a person who may or not be real? He hoped not.

He turned back to the party, listening to the sounds of laughter and yelling and a radio playing from someone's car. He was done with Liz. Just done.

But before he headed back, he looked out at the bridge one last time.

Was there someone standing on the bridge itself? It looked like a woman in a dress. Was that Liz?

Why was she out on the bridge all by herself when everyone knew the story of how Cody died? She had to know the story too. There was no way that she grew up without hearing it if she were in Franklin. It was a tragedy, and maybe the biggest thing to happen to the city ever.

Brendan kept looking out. The woman seemed to glow in the moonlight. It was odd. He didn't think that Liz had been that pale. Or maybe she always had been. He couldn't tell. Now looking out at the bridge and the figure who stood there, staring back at him, he couldn't say that he remembered much about how Liz looked even though he had obsessed about a profile picture she had for a while. And he had stalked her Facebook so thoroughly before this weekend that he could've drawn the freckles across her nose from memory.

But this had to be Liz, right? It had to be. She had texted him. But why was she out there, especially when she had to know that Cody Dempsey had slipped right from that point and fallen into the river? Hadn't the newspaper stories said he died on impact? What the fuck was she thinking?

———

BETTY LEE DIDN'T LOOK DOWN until she was right around the middle of the trestle bridge. She regretted it immediately.

Her knees wobbled and she couldn't find her balance again. She tried looking directly up, but that seemed to make it worse. Her heartbeat faster and her breath came in short gasps. She had never been so scared in her life.

That's when a quiet part of her brain took over. It was the part that kept its cool and made sure she did the thing she needed to do to survive. It was how she got out of trouble most of the time, and it was the part of her brain that was helping her figure out a plan. It was the part of her brain that helped her run away the first time, and it was the part of her brain that got her out on the tracks in the first place.

Her breathing slowed, and she looked directly across the bridge, at the place where her feet would touch land again. She knew she could do it. She knew she could get there.

But what she hadn't counted on was that she would be found so easily.

Though she hadn't remembered seeing a single soul that morning, she could hear voices behind her now, calling her name. She tried to think about anyone she may have passed, but she had been in such a trance that morning. She had been trying to hop a train. She must have missed it. Someone must've seen her come to the railyard.

She turned around to look at the voices on the other side. Her parents were there, quiet and wringing their hands, no doubt embarrassed by their daughter, causing another scene that would reflect poorly on them. There was also the sheriff, and the railyard foreman. Then, beyond them, a group of folks looked on. They were in their Sunday clothes, like they had come from church. Or skipped it all together just to see the commotion.

Well, it didn't matter. Betty turned to look back at the other side of the bridge and took a few more steps. She'd be on the other side soon enough and it would take a long time for them to find her. They'd have to drive out to the Bauman Street bridge, and that was fifteen miles west. Then, they'd have to cross the bridge, drive another fifteen miles back toward the trestle bridge, and by then she could be long gone. She didn't know much about what was on the other side of the bridge, only that it led into the city of Watkins, which was big enough for her to hide in if she needed to. She could make that happen.

With renewed determination, she took another few steps, pausing after each one to make sure she had her balance. And as she continued toward her destination, she could see dust picking up at the other side of the bridge as a Watkins police car pulled up at the other side.

———

BRENDAN COULDN'T HEAR the party anymore. He didn't remember taking the first few steps out onto the bridge, but he had. And by the time he realized he was out on the trestle bridge, he didn't seem to mind. It was like he was meant to be there. Like he was supposed to meet Liz there a long time ago.

They planned it for weeks using AIM. They chatted about it every single night. But weren't they going to meet by the bridge? He couldn't quite remember.

And the night that he was supposed to meet her was the night that Cody died by going out on the bridge by himself and falling. Had Liz seen it happen?

She never said. In fact, Brendan couldn't remember chatting with her at all after it happened. The summer after graduation was a whirlwind of packing for college and working at minimum wage.

He hadn't thought much about Liz until she started messaging him again.

But she stood there now, barefoot on the bridge, halfway out. Her hair was cropped short, about chin length. And her dress seemed like something vintage and cool, like something an interesting woman would've found online. She stood there, looking at him, occasionally turning to look at the other side of the bridge, as if she wanted him to follow her all the way across.

"Liz?" He called out.

She turned back to look at him and didn't say anything.

———

BETTY LEE WAS COMPLETELY out of options. The quiet part of her brain that made plans was silent, as if it were trying to cook up just one more notion. But she couldn't. There was nothing left for her to do. She could turn back and face her parents, and the shame of knowing that everyone in Franklin was casually watching from the railyard like she was some kind of circus performer and not an absolutely desperate girl.

Or she could keep going and meet up with whoever the officer was on the Watkins side of the bridge. Maybe he knew a place where a girl in her situation could get a little bit of help.

But the more she looked at him, the more she knew that wasn't the case. He stood smug on the other side of the bridge, his arms crossed, sometimes one hand wandering to the gun on his hip like it was a security blanket. He was an older man, maybe older than her dad. And he wasn't smiling. He was most likely irritated that someone had ruined his Sunday morning breakfast.

Betty Lee was stuck.

Hell. She'd been stuck since the minute she laid eyes on James. That worthless bastard. She'd thought she was in love. And maybe she had been. Maybe she still was. But if that was love, and if it led to this, well. She was done.

She looked back over her shoulder to the Franklin side of the bridge. She could see her parents. They stood there, silent. Her mother looked at Betty Lee and just quietly shook her head before coming to rest her face on her husband's shoulder.

Her mother couldn't even watch.

That settled it.

The quiet part of Betty Lee's brain was done making plans. There were no more plans to be made. She stood up straight, as straight as she could. She wasn't particularly tall, but she threw her shoulders back and glared at folks gathered on the Franklin side.

Some of them had been friends, she thought, but they certainly weren't any more. But that was okay. She didn't need friends like that. And where she was going, she didn't need anyone.

She stepped off the wooden railroad tie and balanced both her feet on the rail itself. It took a moment for her balance to kick in, and her bare feet still hurt. She waited until both her mother and father looked directly at her, and jumped.

———

THE RIVER WAS SO CALM down below. Brendan couldn't figure out why he'd been so scared to get on the bridge in the first place. And he could see why Liz stood there. She seemed content, like she'd always been on that bridge, and like that bridge was where she belonged.

He wanted to talk to her, to ask her so many questions. He'd completely forgotten Sarah. He'd forgotten that he was supposed to bring her a beer and then head back to the hotel with her. He forgot that he had just in the past few hours developed a crush on her.

But on the bridge, it didn't matter. It was quiet and calm. Crickets and cicadas chirped around the river, and their sound echoed between the banks. The moon was bright and reflected off the water below.

Without thinking, Brendan looked at Liz. "I love you," he said.

He didn't know why. But it didn't matter. It had been meant to be, hadn't it? And now, they were going to be together forever.

Liz wrapped her arms around Brendan, leaning in for a kiss.

At first, Brendan felt nothing. It didn't feel like kissing a person. It felt like he was floating, like he'd just gone to the dentist and was being put under. But it didn't last. There was a coldness. Something wasn't right. What had originally felt like soft lips on his slowly turned rubbery and seemed to disintegrate at the touch.

Where was he? Where was Sarah?

Brendan opened his eyes.

Liz, the woman who only moments before had been a beautiful, shining reflection of moonlight was no more. In his arms was the gray, decaying body of a woman. Bits of decomposing flesh hung off exposed bone. There was no person, just a mass of organic tissue that had been breaking down since before he was even born.

He was falling.

He could see the bridge above him.

He could feel the air rushing past him.

This corpse weighed him down.

He screamed for help once before he hit the water, knowing that he wouldn't be heard over the sound of someone's car stereo playing a late nineties top 40 satellite radio station, and all the laughter and talk of the crowd at the party.

The Black Cat

Kathryn Trattner

Part One - Dollhouse

June brought summer and a black cat. Not the kind you buy at the fireworks stand as you prepare for the Fourth of July—that fearsome face and open maw, red eyes, white fangs. The black cat that came into my life was small and mild, willing enough to be held and petted, carried around in the crook of my arm as I moved between the playhouse in the backyard to the dollhouse in my bedroom. One life sized, the other a miniature; my interior and outer worlds.

Onyx, as sleek and beautiful as the gemstone, green eyes alert and focused. I don't remember where he came from that summer. He was there, as if he'd always been there, a bowl of kibble in the kitchen and a litter box in the garage. I'd never asked for a pet, my mother hadn't inquired if I'd wanted one. Yet our lives were suddenly filled with the sound of the can opener whirring and his matching purr, the black body moving through the house at night, coming to lay at the foot of my bed when I slept.

He was my shadow, a companion through the hot days, a silent playmate as I served invisible tea in plastic cups. Once he let me put him in a pink ruffled baby doll dress, ears laid back, tail twitching, a time bomb tick-tick-ticking.

At night I would stand at the back door, calling his name, my mother calling mine, our voices blurring into one as bedtime was announced.

"Onyx!"

"Maria!"

"It's time for bed!"

The backyard was a tangle of plants, the forgotten space of a previous gardener, shrubs and flowering trees, paths that wound beneath and through it all. My mother had rented the house for this garden, a *magical* place for a little girl to spend her afternoons. At night, filled with the rustle of nocturnal creatures, it was something else. I didn't like to be outside when the sun went down. I could feel how small I was out there, under the stars, with nothing around or above my head. I kept my feet on the cement step, one hand on the door frame, leaning out, calling until I thought he'd never come.

Then Onyx would appear, trotting smoothly out of the darkness, into the yellow glow thrown by the porch light beside the door.

A cat.

A small black cat.

Nothing more.

———

THE DOLL WAS BLONDE, hair an unnatural shade, pink lips, blue eyeshadow. Sometimes when my mother went out, which was rare, she wore the same color—frosted and cool-toned, bringing out the azure in her green eyes.

Once I'd snuck into her room while a babysitter talked on the phone, pressed a single finger into the pan of color, swiping across my own eyelids. I admired myself in her dressing table mirror, the way I suddenly looked so adult, sophisticated and worldly. I forgot to wipe it away before my mother returned, half asleep in my room when I felt the cold washcloth, panicking awake as she gently removed the makeup—rich, heavy perfume filling the air.

I wasn't told to keep out of it, not scolded or warned. She brought me my own the next day. "You're too young to wear makeup, Maria. But you can play with it as much as you like at home."

From then on I'd swipe shimmery blue across my face, Onyx watching as I did. Once I added some to his face, dropping a kiss on soft fur. He washed it off as soon as I pulled away, tail twitching, back turned to me. I added it only to my dolls after that, their faces faintly blue and sparkling, as they went about their lives in the pink dollhouse in the corner of my bedroom.

Three floors and an elevator, cardboard walls covered in stickers to make it appear as if the rooms were filled with furniture and a kitchen. I had pink plastic beds, a table and chairs, a bathtub that I filled carefully with water and bubbles, dolls stripping down to soak and read the carefully folded construction paper books I made. I mimicked my mother. The way I wanted to be when I grew up, when I could sip a golden drink from a cup shaped like a tulip, and read books where women with flowing hair and beautiful dresses were embraced by handsome men.

Onyx stayed close, watching the movement of my hands intently, basking in the sun coming through the window, caught in warmth and dust motes. Sometimes I would prop a doll up against his side, pretend that he played with me, that he was a wild beast tamed and loved by a beautiful woman.

A panther as calm as a house cat; something wild domesticated.

———

A COLOR I had no name for—deep and rich, vibrant and dark. Red. Reminding me of scraped knees and paper cuts, the quick flash of a needle at the doctor. But not a color I expected here, in the shadowy hall, in my house in the middle of a hot Sunday afternoon. Buzzing filled my head, my ears thrumming, and I waved my arms around to brush the noise away—sweat prickled along my forehead, scalp itching.

I hesitated, pulled forward—the open door, the red trail leading into the space beyond, out of sight, into my bedroom.

The house was quiet. My mother was outside talking to the older couple across the street. Her name was Maria too. So many of us, wandering out in the world, connected by the sound of five letters. I thought about that, thousands of girls, like and unlike me. I thought of that instead of the blood in the hall. I thought of other little girls out in the sunshine, at the beach or riding their bikes down a street.

I would pretend I was another little girl.

A collection of droplets, a few here, a few there. Grouping together as if they were lonely, coming together to keep each other company. It wasn't much blood. Not really. But enough. Enough for me to know that something wasn't right. Enough for me to wonder why my mother hadn't seen it already.

I stood in the doorway of my room, going over each piece, looking for the out-of-place thing. The window blinds were open, pulled all the way to the top, the glass covered in painted plastic sun catchers; flowers and watery paint, the sun shining through them to cast multicolored patches of light across my bed, the carpet littered with toys, and the dollhouse.

Struggling for breath, I gasped, unsure, not knowing, but feeling the wrongness of it all. An unnamable thing. A *thing*. In my bedroom. Where I slept. I turned to my bed, the darkness beneath it, so cool and complete, a wasteland beneath my box springs.

Anything could be under there.

But the blood led to the dollhouse. It stood between the

window and the bed, the front turned to me, the facade printed to look like a real house. Pink brick. Bright green rose bushes. Windows tinted light blue, white reflections painted on them. Vibrant, unreal.

I crept forward, pulled, unable to turn away.

The sun warm on my skin, yellow and blue tinged the carpet beneath my feet, the sound of a lawnmower starting up in the distance as I came around to look at the inside. I stood motionless, going over the interior. All of it so familiar, a known structure, a known place.

The dolls were gone. In their place, sitting in chairs at the table and lying on the bed, were mice. Brown. Small. Long tails. Pink hands and feet. Black eyes open. Some looked whole, untouched, as if they'd come out of the walls to play house and gotten caught—frozen, fearful. Others had puncture wounds, fur bloody, a deflated quality to their bodies, as if air were leaking out like it would from a balloon.

The mouse on the bed was the bloodiest, throat ripped wide, pale raw flesh exposed. The creature's head was almost detached. If I reached out, if I touched it, it would roll away, fall out of the house. My hand twitched, skin crawling. It would be soft. Almost no sound when it hit the floor, blood seeping into the carpet fibers.

Onyx appeared, rubbing against my legs, purring.

I ran from the room, panting, chest tight, leaving him behind. Out through the front door, flying down the steps and across the lawn to where my mother was laughing. Laughing, as if my room weren't full of dead things.

"Mom! Mom!"

She turned to me, still smiling, holding out an arm so that I could squeeze in close, press myself to her hip, feel her arm settle over my shoulders.

"You have to come see."

The neighbors chuckled, the other Maria sharing a look

with her husband, a glance as if they knew what I was talking about.

"You go on in. We'll catch up later," said the other Maria. "Looks like she's got something important to share."

I nodded, swallowing.

"What is it baby?" she asked, following me, a half-smile lingering.

"You just have to see."

I didn't want to tell her. I didn't know what to say, how to explain.

Air conditioning hit us as we came through the front door, the house dim, blinds and curtains pulled over the windows. I hesitated in the entryway, on the tile, searching for more blood.

"Maria," my mother said, voice hardening, an edge of worry creeping in. "What's going on?"

I shook my head, taking her hand, guiding her toward my room. She stopped in the hall, seeing the red droplets. Frowning, forehead wrinkling, brows coming together, she moved me aside, dropping my hand to hurry ahead.

I knew what she would see. The room a rainbow of color, the pink dollhouse, the dark wet spots, the mice. The hall seemed so quiet and dark compared to that space, a reprieve, a safe space. I wanted to stay here, to put off seeing what I knew to be true, the growing horror of it sneaking up behind me, great clawed hands reaching, ready to take me gently by the shoulders.

"Maria," my mother said. Invisible from where I stood, a figment, my name coming from a place I couldn't see. "Come here."

Stepping forward, shoulders back, I entered the room. There was nothing I could say, nothing to explain, she had seen everything I had, she would understand why I'd come running out of the house, desperate to show her something that shouldn't be there.

"Baby, I'm so sorry." She held out her hand, inviting me to cross the distance between us. "Onyx must have brought this in. Sometimes cats do that."

I didn't look down, didn't want to see all of those dead mice sleeping and sitting—pretend dinners and sweet dreams. She seemed so casual, her words soft, nothing anxious or scared. Not the emotions I'd been expecting at all.

"You know," she said, taking my hand. "Cats usually bring you things because they love you and think you're unable to take care of yourself. That you're not grown up enough yet to hunt."

"Because they love you?"

She nodded. "Yeah. He's brought you lunch."

"Lunch?"

"I'll get a bag and get it cleaned up. It'll just take a moment and then it will all be good as new."

A bag? Would that be enough for all of those tiny bodies, the blood all over the printed cardboard and plastic. I sucked in a deep breath, pulling it all the way into my lungs, holding it, my cheeks puffed out, and looked down.

A single mouse. Just the one. Bloody but whole, no missing limbs, the fur wet and matted. It was on the bottom floor of the house. Not in a chair. Not in a bed. Just lying there, as if it had been casually dropped—an offering, a *gift*.

I jumped as something brushed against my leg. Looking down at Onyx as he turned to brush against me again, arching his back, soft fur to bare skin. Soft, so soft. His purr filled the room, vibrating, and he squinted his green eyes as he looked up at me, something like a smile on his cat face.

I love you.

Part Two - Nightmare

The summer days were longer, stretching out, worn thin in places, transparent in the heat. I didn't play with the dollhouse again. My mother had been right, she'd made it good as new. But still. *Still.* I didn't look beyond that word, refusing to pull what I felt into the light, into the direct rays of a summer sun.

I spent more time outside riding my bike down our hill, legs out, pedals spinning, tempted but not daring enough to let go of the handlebars and fly like the other kids on the street. I'd told Samantha—the girl up the street and a friend in the way that neighborhood kids are friends without being close—about the mouse, just the one, no more, and her face had crinkled up, a piece of paper wadded tight. *Gross.* So I didn't mention it again.

I would come home as the night closed in, sweaty and smiling, happy to have spent the day under the cloudless sky. Onyx would be waiting on the front porch, perfectly still, eyes intent, tail wrapped around his feet. He was always there, the first person to greet me when I came home, ready with a meow.

The rest of the time he came and went as he pleased. My mother or I would open the sliding glass door for him—in and out, out and in. He didn't bring me another mouse. Maybe he'd been disappointed when I hadn't eaten it, watching my mother pick it up in a washcloth and throw it in a bag, drop it in the garbage bin outside. *Such a waste.*

He sat and watched us eat dinner at the kitchen table. Salad. Hamburger and noodles. Baked chicken. Tacos. A rotation of things that never included something wild being brought in for dinner. Mice never graced our shatterproof plates.

In the evenings he sat on my mother's lap, the blue light of the television washing over our faces. Purring, eyes closed, he would reach out one paw to me, touching whatever was closest, hand or knee. He was always happiest when he could be touching us both at the same time.

"Alright," my mother said. "Time to get ready for bed.

Brush your teeth and put your pajamas on. We'll read a couple of chapters tonight."

I nodded, hurrying to the bathroom, slathering my toothbrush with bubblegum-flavored toothpaste. None of my other friends were read to at night, grown out of the bedtime story at the age of ten. But my mother continued, the reading level of the books improving as I'd gotten older. We'd long ago surpassed simple chapter books. We'd worked our way through *The Hobbit* and *The Lord of the Rings*. Now we were reading the *Narnia* books— full of magic wardrobes and lions, ships shaped like dragons, dying planets.

Our routine was for me to start first. I'd read until I got tired, passing the book to her. Sometimes we had to reread because I fell asleep as she read. But I didn't mind. I liked the evenings propped up together in my bed beneath the quilt, the bedside table light on, the nightlight across the room glowing. Onyx joined us, inching his way up, squeezing between us and purring gently.

I would fall asleep to the sound of my mother's voice.

———

I COULDN'T BREATHE.

A weight on my chest, so heavy, ribs creaking beneath the pressure, heart throbbing. I was being crushed, pushed through the mattress, down into the foundation of the house, past concrete, into the cold hard earth.

Scream.

I tried. I wanted to. It lodged in my throat. Opening my eyes, coming out of the dream, the pressure on my chest didn't ease, didn't fade. It was just as heavy, just as present. My room was black, the nightlight burnt out, no light on in the hall or the kitchen.

My mother always left a light on for me.

I couldn't move my arms or legs. My lips refused to part.

An unbearable weight. I wasn't going to survive this. Sunshine was over for me. Fruity cereal in the mornings at the kitchen table. Exploring the creek behind our house. Giant frogs and lightning bugs. Blue eyeshadow. My mother's warmth, the way she hugged me tight, kissing the top of my head.

It was all gone.

The purr started then, sinking into muscle and bone, filling me. The weight on my chest easing slightly, enough so that I gasped, pulling in air. Onyx. I knew him now, recognized him in the dark. But he didn't move. He continued to sit on me, purring in the dark, an endless thrumming in my head.

I felt a paw, the tips of claws in the softness, as he touched my face. Gently, tenderly. And then he retreated, lifting off my chest completely, and I felt his weight on the bed beside me, the thump he made as he left it, jumping off the mattress and landing on the floor. I listened, the purr continuing, retreating down the hall.

Part Three - Locket

I was twelve when a new family moved in on our street. A girl my age, my grade. Diana. Named after a princess, a dead woman, but looking nothing like her. This girl had white-blonde hair, cut short in a sharp bob, eyes so blue it hurt to look into them.

We'd walked home together, talking about the gym teacher we shared, the kids in our separate homerooms. A tentative friendship, something fresh to go along with the new school year—new clothes, white sneakers. I was still feeling it out, trying to navigate my way into it.

At my house, while my mother worked toward the end of her day, we ate cappuccino chocolate ice cream out of blue bowls and watched the last thirty minutes of daytime television—heavily made-up women and dramatic lighting, music over it all, clinging like perfume.

"Got a bathroom?"

"Sure." I pointed with my spoon. "Down the hall and on the right."

She'd excused herself, going back to the restroom, leaving me to scrape out the last few pieces of chocolate clinging to the side of my blue bowl. Then she was back, in a hurry to leave, backpack over a shoulder and already at the front door.

"I'll see you tomorrow, okay?" I smiled at her, question and declaration all in one.

"Yeah, okay."

After putting our bowls in the sink and shaking cat kibble into Onyx's red dish I wandered back to my room. I had homework to do. Math. Spelling. But I wanted to lay on my bed with a book by Patricia C. Wrede more than I wanted to expand myself in other directions. Dragons, a princess, and talking cats were better companions.

The box on my dresser was open. Simple, carved wood, scrolls and almost flowers, something that must have been mass-produced but precious to me. A place to keep the things I valued, treasures secreted away, hoarded for a day I would need them.

My stomach sank. It had been picked through, gone over, junk and debris to the searcher, finding very little worth taking. A bracelet. A pair of snap-on shimmery earrings made of glass. A gold-plated heart-shaped locket.

"No, no, no!"

I dumped the contents on the floor, sinking down, spreading it all out. I had to be sure. I could have missed the glitter, a hint of gold, a reflection of light. Tears pooled in my eyes and fell, a sob coming up from my gut. It was more than the stolen items. A loss. Friendship offered with one hand and taken away with another.

Snot touched my upper lip, the room blurry around me, and I let out a howl of grief. No one else was here. My mom wouldn't ask questions, wouldn't peel away the band-aid to poke at the rawness of this wound. I couldn't face telling her about the missing locket, a Christmas gift, our photos together inside.

A soft body touched me, small and silky, Onyx making a questioning sound. I jumped, startled, blinking tears away to see him clearly. He looked from my face to the pile in front of me, my hands balled into the carpet.

"Oh, Onyx," I sobbed, picking him up and burying my face in his fur. "Diana took the locket Momma gave me."

He began to purr, warm in my arms, the sound growing, filling my head and sinking into my bones. I wanted to go back to ice cream and walks home, to someone I'd thought was my friend.

———

MORE WAS GONE than just the locket. She'd stolen a bracelet—a purple ring, glitter trapped in clear plastic, large enough that it would slip off if I wasn't paying attention. *Pay attention.* And two sparkly clip-on earrings. I didn't tell my mom. I didn't want her to know that I'd lost the locket after she'd told me how important it was to hold on to.

The next morning, quiet over breakfast, I pretended to be sick. My stomach hurt. But it wasn't much of a lie. My mom, in a hurry to get to the office on time, promised she'd call to check on me. There were cartoons and cereal until the quiet afternoon and Onyx on the sofa beside me. He lapped up the leftover milk, licking his whiskers, cleaning a paw.

When it was time I got dressed quickly, hurrying to beat the bus, fast walking to Diana's house—Diana the thief, Diana the backstabber. Onyx followed but somewhere along the way I lost him, or he lost me, and when I reached her backyard— silver chain-link fence, green garbage cans, tan siding and red brick—I was alone.

I didn't have to wait long, jittery with expectation. She

came around the corner of the house, swinging a yellow backpack around and humming, the purple bracelet flashing on her wrist. When she saw me, she stopped, face reddening. I held out my hand, palm up, waiting.

"You took my locket, Diana. I want it back."

"I didn't take anything from you."

I began to shake, hurt and wounded, heart pounding, tears threatening.

"You were in my room!"

"I don't know what you're talking about." A sneer on her face, denial and lie, determined to stick to it all.

Diana tried to move past me. I blocked the gate, holding onto it, trying to stop her from walking away. I gripped the chain-link fence, desperate, my cheeks wet with tears.

"Get out of the way!"

"I want my locket!" Begging, pleading, wishing so hard my heart hurt. I wanted the necklace back. I wanted to pretend this hadn't happened. "I thought you were my friend."

"You're stupid, Maria! You're stupid and I hate you!"

"Please, Diana!"

"Get out of the way!"

Diana kicked me, white sneaker against my bare leg, tearing the skin, blood welling up. I faltered, fell away, the chain-link rattling, the gate unguarded. She ran past me and into her house, taking the purple bracelet with her.

———

THE PHONE in the kitchen rang—beige plastic, extra-long spiral cord.

"Maria, would you get that please?"

I jumped up from the sofa, abandoning Saturday morning cartoons, and ran to the phone, catching it mid-ring.

"Hello?"

"Hello?" An echo of my own word but somber, heavy across the buzzing line. "Is this Maria?"

I made an affirmative noise.

"Can I talk to your mom, honey?"

"Sure," I said, turning to my mom at the sink elbow deep in soapy dishes, and held out the phone. "It's for you."

With a sigh she wiped her hands and came to take it. "Hello? Yes. Oh! Annette, hi. I didn't recognize your voice for a second. What's going on?"

I watched her face fall, the friendliness and warmth dropping, the somberness of the voice on the other end of the line overtaking her, changing her. My mom's eyes fell on me, an unreadable expression, one never seen before. Something like fear, horror, terrible sadness.

"Hold on just a second," she said, covering the mouth piece with a hand. "Go play in the backyard for a little bit, okay?"

———

IT WAS in the playhouse waiting for me. My shin scabbed and bruised still from Diana's tough sneakers, the kick with so much anger behind it. I could still feel the chain-link fence in my hands, desperation in my heart. How fragile my idea of friendship. How easily it proved false.

I'd come to hide, clutching a book and glass of water, not minding if the space is filled with spiders. No door. Simple square for windows. A child-size table and chairs. Dim in the back, the light not reaching all the way in, not touching the deep corners—rough wooden walls, weather-worn.

A sparkle on the table caught my eye. A beacon. A silent screaming object.

I paused watching it, as if it could move, as if legs might sprout and it would scuttle away. *Move.* Because if it moved that meant it wasn't real. A trick of the light. A game played by shadows. A shard of nightmare coming into the day, something to blink away, rub from my eyes like sleep.

An ear. Small. Pale. A shiny clip-on earring attached.

My earring.

Cicadas sang, droning love songs into the air. The sun on my back hot through thin cotton. The book in my hand wawas light, the cover glossy, the pages within the recycled brown color of cheap paper. No shoes. I'm half in, half out, my toes on the bare boards of the floor, heels in the dirt outside.

I am between two places and holding on to everything outside the pretend house for all I'm worth.

But it's inevitable that I will go inside. It's coming and I can't stop it.

So I step forward to meet it.

The other earring is there too. The purple bracelet and gold locket. I don't reach for them, I don't touch them. But I want to. I want to know if the photos of my mother and I are still inside, our photographed faces pressed together, kissing in the closed off darkness of metal heart.

I lick my lips, mouth dry, forgetting the water in my hand, the book. And now I know I'm not alone. It wasn't here the moment before, the area all mine, mine to scream and cry in without a witness. But I can feel it waiting, watching.

"Maria!"

The glass shatters at my feet and I take a stumbling step back. Several pieces of the glass lodge in the bottoms of my feet and I scream, falling back on my butt, the book flying away. The pain intense. I can hear my mom running, voice high, as blood seeps into the dirt, my feet on fire.

Through tears, I see something shift in the dim interior of the playhouse.

———

LATER, my mom brings the jewelry inside and returns it to the cheap box on my dresser. She doesn't ask why it was there. It doesn't matter. What matters are the cuts in the soles of my feet—how soon they might heal, how I would go to school and if she could get the time off work to take care of me.

I want to ask her about the ear. I want to know if she saw the blood, the small pale piece of human flesh in the playhouse, in our back garden, in our lives. Did she remove one sparkling earring, clean it off, and put it back?

Instead, she tells me about the phone call, voice serious, concerned eyes searching my face. Diana is missing. It was her mother on the phone, the worried Annette. The police want any information about the last time she was seen. I swallow the lump in my throat, terrible certainty filling me. My mouth begins to water, nausea setting in.

"Diana went missing after school yesterday. Have you seen her? Her mom said she was here a few days ago, she said you guys watched some tv and ate ice cream. Have you seen her since then?"

The ear. The false glittering earring. The shadow moving in the corner.

"No."

Part Four - The Doctor

A blank room like a canvas, ready for whatever might happen, whatever it might contain. Anything could happen in a room like this. Beneath me paper crinkled, bleached white, sterile. I looked down at my nails, chewed down to the quick, cuticles raw, and I had to stop myself from picking at them, peeling tiny strips of skin away; the satisfaction it brought, the small point of pain—forgetfulness, distraction.

Beyond the door I could hear the whispered conversation; my mother's voice tense but rising, the doctor a monotone calm. This wasn't my regular doctor, the one I went to for rashes and colds, her office was brightly colored; bright blue and green halls, the rooms I waited in purple and red, flowers and artwork done by other kids. I'd given her a drawing once, the two of us together with her handing me a band-aid. It had still been there on my last visit.

Doctor Richardson had suggested my mom take me here. A card handed over gripped tight, my mom's hand trembling; red nails, a gold ring with a pale green sparkling stone.

Doctor Alvarez, a man with very serious eyes and no hair, asked me questions while my mom filled out stacks of paper-work. Yes and no questions, little dots she filled in with a pencil, a focused, determined expression on her face.

"Do you have nightmares?"

"Do you feel anxious? Worried?"

The questions went on and I answered as best I could. A little hesitant, not wanting to give away too much. I needed to keep myself pulled in tight, elbows close to my body, hands clasped in my lap, ankles crossed.

I didn't tell him about the pale pink ear, the bloody mice. The weight on my chest in the middle of a pitch--black night.

It was the information he was after. The reason my mom had brought me here without knowing it. She thought it was Diana. Stress. Fear. *What if?*

"A girl on our street went missing last week, a friend. They haven't found her. And there's something wrong with Maria. She jumps a mile high if I startle her. I know it doesn't seem like much. I know it. But I know my daughter, something has changed."

Grief. Shock. These were the reasons she was given, a book to teach us both coping mechanisms, the suggestion of medication. Pills in a transparent orange bottle, white safety cap, with my name in harsh black letters on the label; warn-ings, directions. And a list of names for someone I could talk to once a week.

The car ride home was quiet. I glanced at her once, tall

enough to sit in the front seat now, the car behind us long and hollow. I wished I'd sat in the back, behind her so I wouldn't have to look at her, watching the world roll by, imagining a black cat racing us, keeping pace on the verge of the highway. But her silence, the way it spread out between us, made it impossible to ignore.

———

"YOU KNOW you can talk to me, baby? You know that right?"

I nodded. "Yeah, of course."

"Anything you need, I'll help you with. I'll listen, it doesn't matter what time it is or where. I'll be there for you. Always."

"I know. I love you, Mom."

"Okay," she said, pulling me into a tight hug. Squeezing me, her head buried in my shoulder, holding onto me as if she could keep whatever haunted me away.

Behind her, walking out of the kitchen, Onyx watched us with curious green eyes.

Part Five - Birds

There is a cliché about lonely children. Everything happens to them; horrors and adventures, the glint of destiny on steel, a kiss that changes the world. I was that child without the call to something greater. I played with dolls until I was too old, kept books close, walked with my eyes down through hallways filled with lockers and voices raised to reach the ceiling.

The few friends I had seemed to fade away over time. There were no sleepovers and gossip, no painted nails while names were tossed around, crushes and broken hearts being exchanged. The boyfriends I picked up were never anyone I brought home to meet my mother. Kisses in parked cars, sweaty hands, fumbling, tumbling, coming together and falling apart.

After it all, at the end of days or nights, months or years, Onyx waited.

How long did I know I lived with a monster? My monster? I'd heard stories about creatures living beneath beds, inhabiting closets, and small dark spaces. The boogeyman; a myth, a *legend*. It took a long time to admit it to myself, in the quiet of my mind, in a place filled with sunshine and silence. I never said it out loud. My mom never believed in monsters. Not real. Not a part of our reality. But even as small as I was then I knew that didn't mean we weren't a part of theirs.

I carried that thought, that idea, with me into adulthood.

And Onyx followed me there.

Not all childhoods are magical. Sometimes, as you grow up—up and up until there is nowhere else for you to go but out of the house, out into the world—you look back and see the flaws.

It was a single--parent house, my mother working late into the evenings, as I let myself in the house after school, remembering to set the frozen chicken on the counter to thaw. I did homework at the kitchen table alone, watched television and read. Sat out in the backyard, watching the night come on, stars and lightning bugs filling the sky, waiting for the bolt on the front door to turn, for Mom to call out to me.

"Maria!"

I still hear her voice.

Onyx was there when she passed, splitting his time between my tiny apartment in town and my mother's house. I would drop him off for long weekends or stretches during the week. A kind of joint custody that he seemed to prefer.

At first, I'd taken him with me. But he sat at the door and howled, inconsolable until he saw her again. She said after a few days with her, he did the same thing at her house. And when she'd been in the hospital and he'd yowled for her I asked the nurse if I could bring him to visit. She'd looked at me strangely, but nodded. I carried him up in my arms, calm and patient.

When she passed I was holding her hand and Onyx was purring.

———

ORPHAN.

All alone in the world. It felt strange to know I'd never see my mom again, never hold her hand or eat dinners cooked with love—favorite things, comfort foods. But not really alone. Onyx was there too.

How long do cats live? Living their nine lives, separate from you as they go out into the world, beyond the open door, passing by you without a backward glance. Did they still belong to you then? I wondered sometimes if other people left food on back porches, ran their hands along his back to scratch the base of his tail. But he always came back to me, sitting close, reaching out to touch me with one paw to let me know I belonged to him.

He went out less when she was gone, came back sooner, cut his outside life short. I think he could feel I needed him more, needed someone to help me bear the silence of the apartment, the loneliness that overtook me, the tears.

I had to remind myself where I was. College. Working toward a degree in business. Classes were a blur, kind professors extending due dates, the dean stopping by to offer condolences in her calm, impersonal way. My boss at the restaurant where I waited tables was less understanding, letting me know I could take some time but needed to come back soon. There was no money coming in, the small life insurance check only covered the cremation expenses. The cat food supply began to dwindle and slowly the fridge began to empty, the cabinets holding noodles and not much else.

Then the birds began to arrive.

———

I DON'T KNOW where he found the variety. Cardinal. Wren. Oriole. Robin. Finch. Others I couldn't identify. I could have looked them up, run my finger down glossy bird books, but I couldn't face that. I didn't want to know if they were rare. If he had made them rarer.

I tried to keep him in at night, making sure the deadbolt was in place. Then I tried a chair and moved a small table to block the only way in and out.

Nothing worked.

———

A BLUE JAY—BLUE and white, crested, feet curled up, grasping an invisible branch. He lay on the cement in front of the door. I watched it, waiting for the feet to uncurl, an eye to blink. Any sign of life. An ant arrived, sensing death and dinner, forging a path for others to follow.

I moved it to a bush on the side of the building, tucking it beneath the branches, out of the sun. Maybe it would have liked it there. Maybe that's where it had come from. The ant crawled on top of my hand and I gently blew it off, hoping it would find what it was looking for again.

———

"ONYX, I'M HOME!"

But he was already there, the jingle of my keys in the door alerting him, the freedom of the world beyond this tiny space calling. He was through my legs and trotting away before I could stop him. Off to do cat things and live his best cat life.

"Nice to see you too," I said as he disappeared around the corner.

I'd let him in later, when he came back to scratch at the door sometime in the middle of night. Or he'd come to the bedroom window and meow until I got up, strolling inside as if he'd never been gone.

I shut the door and set my bag down, blowing out a sigh, brain mush from a full day of classes and back sore from being on my feet at the restaurant for another five hours afterward. My stomach ached with emptiness but I was tired enough to choose sleep over food. Exhausted, burning the candle at both ends, praying that I wouldn't fizzle out. I wasn't sure I'd be able to light myself again.

Stumbling to the bedroom I took off my jeans, shimmying out of them, tossing them with my foot to a pile by the bed. I smelled like fried foods—cheese, pickles, chicken, and ranch dressing. It permeated my skin, my hair, getting under my nails. But I didn't care right now. I took everything else off and crawled into bed, pulling the quilt up, and falling asleep almost instantly.

I woke to a rough tongue going over my face, smelly cat kisses, the always purr. Onyx, heavy paws on my shoulder, leaning into me, determined to wake me up. I opened one eye, squinting at him, his face close to mine, green eyes, black whiskers tickling.

I glanced at the bedside clock. Just after five in the morning. My alarm would be going off soon anyway, the first class at seven, the ones that came after, a few hours at the library to work on my paper, and following all of that work, jaw already aching from the demanded friendly smile.

Onyx meowed, the sound pitiful and hungry.

But when had I let him inside? I didn't remember getting up, even shuffling to the door half--asleep to let him back in. There had been no meow beyond the window. Nothing. He jumped off the bed, hurrying away, meowing as he went.

"Alright," I said. "I'm getting up. I'll open you a can."

Small cans with pop lids, peeled back, the juices inside sometimes flicking out. I didn't want to know what cat food was made of. Fish. Chicken. Beef. Deep down I didn't believe it. I'd heard about the pet food documentaries but never watched them. I might try to train my cat to be a vegetarian otherwise.

I was half asleep still—a lingering dream, the memory of pressure on my chest, then the sudden pull back to consciousness as a rough tongue touched my cheek. The can was light, a nothing weight in my hand, as I turned to get a plate from the cabinet. It dropped, hitting the tile floor, clattering, rolling away.

A sparrow, small and brown, a pattern of delicate shades —a curl of winter leaf or rough rolled bark. It lay on the plate, a knife and fork beside it. Limp. Lifeless. Dead. My skin prickled, cold and then heat touching me, rolling through me as my stomach clenched.

The knife and fork caught the reflection of the overhead kitchen light. The plate was my mother's, something I'd taken from the house of my childhood, carried into my adulthood. It was wrong, to have it tinged with death like this, to carry such a delicate meal.

I looked down at him, meeting a steady green gaze.

My mother had said a cat will try to feed you. It sees you as another cat, a stupid cat unable to feed yourself, and will bring you meals until you're able to hunt on your own. Onyx jumped onto the counter and began to purr.

"I don't eat birds," I said, my voice small, coming from a distant place.

The purr stopped. He watched me.

"You know you're not allowed on the counter." I picked him up, heavy and warm, all solid muscle in my arms. I set him on the floor, smoothing his ears down, his eyes closing for a moment.

Leave it. Face it later. Conquer your day first, do the things that must be done. I bent and picked up the can, tapping it onto a plate, gelatinous and uniform. I left the sparrow on the counter, unable to touch it, something in me revolting, closing off.

Onyx rubbed against my leg, the smell of cat food strong in the room, fishy and foul.

He followed me around the apartment, in and out of the bathroom, the closet looking for my favorite t-shirt. A shadow. A companion. When I left the apartment, pulling the door closed, holding the key and ready to lock it, I caught a glimpse of him jumping onto the sofa and settling down for a bath.

When I came home from work the dead thing in my apartment was gone. The dish sat in the drying rack, the knife and fork put up.

Part Six - Shadow

Awake.

Thick darkness lay over me, heavy like a blanket weighted down for reassurance. This was the opposite of that. Crushing. Something about it familiar, recalling times when I'd woken to find Onyx on my chest, purring into the night, pinning me to the bed.

Something else kept me in place now.

My heart raced, chest tight, instant fight or flight. Pure panic. But where? Where could I go? Why did I need to go? I fought to penetrate the darkness, searching blindly, listening. Pitch--black, no light, no noise. But I could feel it. I was being watched.

Slowly my eyes adjusted, shapes coming forward, as if appearing through mist, fuzzy and indistinct. The bedroom door was open. Had it been closed? I usually kept it closed, needing the security, the moment it would give me if a stranger entered my house.

I moved my legs, searching for Onyx, the warmth of him at the foot of my bed; a comforting presence.

Nothing.

He'd been there as I'd given into sleep, silently asking the universe to gift it dreamlessly, to hold the confused prophecies that would never come true, the strangeness of stop motion time. No memories tonight. No last words or jumbled sentences. I had pleaded for it and it had been answered. But coming back from that place left me slow, head thick, full of sleep.

"Onyx?" I whispered.

Something moved in the hall, feet on carpet, shuffling, coming toward me. Not a small thing. A hulking shape filled the doorframe, darkness within darkness. Huge. Coming when I called, answering me. Faintly glowing green eyes fixed on me, farther up than possible, near the ceiling, reflective like animal eyes.

I sat up, a scream lodged in my throat, a choking sound, and fumbled with my bedside lamp. I could hear it, *please, please, please.* Soft, desperate. The light snapped on, bright light blinding me, relief and fear coming at the same time. Now I would see it, now I would know.

The pleading came from me, soft and raspy, but I didn't recognize my own voice. I bit the tip of my tongue, stopping the words, focusing on the pressure. The creature would be there when I turned, when I looked back to the doorway, filling the opening, waiting to step fully into the light. Forcing myself, everything inside of me screaming, I turned to the door.

A small black cat. Green eyes. Tail wrapped around his paws, perfectly still.

Onyx.

We sat staring at each other.

All of my life he kept coming out the dark, through locked doors, from back gardens and dim halls. I looked beyond him, to the hall and the long shadows. The outline of a hulking shape, a sharp snout and curved horns, spines along a curved back, and a tail. It moved, shifting on its feet, hands limp at its side, with thin clawed fingers.

It was all so clear, as if the shadow being cast was the thing itself.

Onyx yawned, eyes squinting, a flash of sharp white teeth, a pinkish-red tongue.

My cat. The friend of my childhood. My companion.

"Come here," I said, patting the mattress.

An invitation, welcoming, accepting the monster in my house.

He came, a small sound coming from him, pleasure at being invited in and wanted.

When he jumped on the bed it dipped as if he weighed more, the small body dense with muscle, bones of iron or steel. I reached forward, running my hand over his head, smoothing down his ears. He closed his eyes, content, enjoying the attention and came toward me, leaning into the contact.

The light remained on as I eased back, pulling the quilt up as he settled down beside my hip purring contentedly. I kept running my hand over his head, down his back, his fur so soft and glossy.

I slept with the light on after that. A grown woman afraid of the dark.

Part Seven - Keys

"Hold the elevator!"

A hand shot between the closing doors, an arm following, the man pushing inside the small space. My finger hovered over the button that closed the doors, not quick enough to beat him to it. I didn't look at him. No eye contact as I hit the button for the fourth floor of the parking garage where my car waited.

"What floor?" I asked.

"Fourth."

I nodded, adjusting my purse on my shoulder, running an inventory of the contents. Keys. Wallet. Cell phone. Sunglasses. Gum. There was pepper spray in my car, slipped beneath the seat. I kept meaning to fish it out but I hadn't. *Too late.*

The man moved to stand behind me. I could just see him out of the corner of my eye. Tall. Dark hair. Jeans and a t-shirt. He was on his phone, scrolling, seeming to ignore me. But my skin crawled.

The elevator rose, rumbling, shimmying up the shaft. I'd had the last appointment of the day. The monthly visit with my psychiatrist. Yes, the medication was working. Yes, my nightmares and anxiety were under control. I'd had to park on the top level, the ceiling low, cars squeezed into tiny slots. But it would be emptier now. Empty.

With a ding the elevator stopped, the red number four above the door as it slid open. I hesitated, waiting for the stranger to walk past me, to prove me wrong, to go on about his life.

"Go ahead," he said.

I smiled tightly, eyes down, death grip on my purse as I stepped from metal floor to cement. Walk calmly. Casual. *You're not in any danger.* My keys jingled as I pulled them out, the sound echoing, filled with promise. I couldn't see my car from here but I knew it was there. Small red car, just around the corner. A few cars still waiting for their owners. Black sedans. Mini vans. Huge trucks with thick tires.

Footsteps followed me. Right there, so close. I glanced back, over a shoulder, making a fist around my keys. The man was looking down at his phone, scrolling still, reading something as he walked. Texts. News. Memes. He wanted nothing from me. But I looked too long and he felt my eyes, his gaze flicking up, dark eyes meeting mine.

Nothing there. Nothing human. *Nothing. Nothing. Nothing.*

Cold swept through me, stomach dropping. Fear, my familiar, my friend returned. *I've missed you.* I began to walk faster, looking forward now, hearing him speed up, our footsteps matching, marching in time, filling my ears. A huge truck was blocking the view of my car, I knew it was there—a bubble of safety.

This wasn't going to happen. I pressed the key fob, the car beeping, lights flashing. I could feel the lock sliding home already, I knew the pressure of the driver's seat beneath me, the seat belt clicking. A scream was crawling up my throat but my mouth was dry, my chest too tight to pull enough air in to make it happen, to let it escape.

The footsteps behind me grew louder, covering more distance, sneakers on concrete, swift and sure. I did scream finally. Pushing it out, the strangled sound nothing like the wail I'd hoped for, a loud piercing call that might bring someone to me, that might save me. A dry yelp. Weak. But my car was just there, on the other side of the huge truck. I could see the rear end, the shelter it promised.

My shoe hit something, a crack in the pavement, a tiny stone, a nothing. I pitched forward, landing hard on my knees, my hands out to catch me—stinging, the bite of bruised and broken flesh. The man was almost there, almost on me, the sound of him closing in felt in my bones. *This is it.* I tensed, solid stone, waiting. I squeezed my eyes shut, panting, ready for his hands to land on me, for his breath to hit my neck, for the world to go dark. I would fight. I would get up and run any second. But my muscles were locked.

Please no.

A noise like a meat tenderizer hitting a cheap cut of beef. My mother came to mind, the image of her standing in the kitchen and making chicken fried steaks, a small silver hammer with a spiked surface smacking into red flesh. Again. Over and over. Potatoes bubbling on the stove, hissing and steaming as the water boiled. She turned to me, the small me, the child inside the adult, and smiled.

It hadn't happened.

I opened my eyes, unclenching my jaw, loosening my body to turn and look behind me. Empty. The parking garage was empty. On shaky legs I stood, turning in a circle, searching the area. I couldn't see him. But there was nowhere for him to go.

My keys were a few feet away, near the truck, close to my car. They'd gone flying when I fell, sliding across the cement. I crossed to them and bent, stopping when something under the truck caught my eye.

A pair of legs was disappearing into the shadows, sliding toward the front of the vehicle, beneath the engine where it was darkest. Jeans. Sneakers. Something wet caught the light, an oil slick, condensation from the air conditioner. Not anything else. Not blood.

My keys jingle-jangled in my hand, stomach turning, feet carrying me to my car without realizing it. The lock I'd so desperately wanted snapping into place. I was out of the spot with a squeal of tires, driving without watching where I was going, eyes on the white truck in the rearview mirror.

Part Eight - End

Greg. Such a normal name. Generic. Greg with his sandy--colored hair and blue eyes, tall enough that I had to look up, stand on tiptoes to kiss him. He never came to me, never reached for me. I was always grasping, always tugging him away from whatever was more important. Everything was more important.

I don't know how I got to the place where he raised his hand. A tense conversation on my sofa, the television volume low, drowned out by raised voices. A muscle in his jaw jumping as I spoke, clenching and unclenching, as more questions came. I wanted commitment, I wanted something more solid than the nights he came to my apartment and left me early in the morning. I wanted something solid beneath my feet and I'd finally reached a point where I was ready to ask for it.

Afterward I told myself I'd known better. When the apartment was dark, ice pressed to my lip, already wondering how I would cover up the swollen eye on Monday morning. After he'd gone. I sat on the kitchen floor, shaking, refusing to cry, wincing and talking to myself.

"You shouldn't have said anything."

"He said he was sorry."

"This is your fault."

Later, after I'd looked in the mirror, and pressed a fingertip to my my lip so hard blood welled up, I cried. Onyx wove between my legs, rubbing against me, head to tail. When I didn't bend down to pet him, he jumped up, landing on the bathroom counter with a thump. He looked at me, waiting for me to pet him, and when I didn't, he put his front paws on my shoulder, leaning into me, sniffing my face.

"It's okay," I said, petting him finally, smoothing back his ears. "I'm fine."

———

A HISSING BREATH, through clenched teeth, sounding tight and drawn out, someone fighting to hold on to it. I could feel it beneath my breastbone, heart constricting, pounding back into life. I swallowed, mouth dry, that same old feeling creeping up, coming to take my hand.

I know you, it said. *Hello friend.*

Setting down the laundry I was folding into neat piles, I stood. The room around me was a mess. Deep cleaning. Scrubbing Greg out of all of it. New sheets. Clothes in plastic bags to give away. I was starting fresh.

The hissing breath came again, traveling through the quiet

air, sounding as if it were on the other side of my closed bedroom door. I steeled myself for it, hand on the knob, letting go a breath of my own before pulling it open.

The hall was dim, a little light from the windows in the living room coming through. For a moment it reminded me of another hall, one from my childhood. The door to the bathroom was barely open, just a sliver of light, home to the harsh breath, the desperation. At the end of the hall, sitting perfectly still, was Onyx.

"What did you bring me?" I whispered.

Terror unfolded, curling out like an opening flower, the curl of a fern frond—perfect and tightly green. The cat blinked at me, slow, and waited for me to see for myself. A low groan came from the bathroom but I couldn't look away from the cat.

He seemed to shrug and gave me a *merp*, stretching as he stood. I clenched my hands, not in anger, but fear, keeping myself from trembling, holding myself so tight. *Don't let go.* Crossing to the bathroom he paused, shot me a look, and pushed the cracked door open, slipping inside.

I followed, called, *summoned*, knowing this was the time that counted the most. Out of all the things that had happened over the years, seen and unseen, this was the one that would change how I looked at the world. I thought it had come so many times before, I thought I'd been here and passed it. No. It was now.

I curled my toes into the carpet as I went, putting my hand flat against the door to push it open, the tile of the room cold as I entered. My face in the mirror startled me—a fading bruise, a scabbed upper lip. My eyes were wide, pupils dilated, ready to take it all in. Expectation. Impending doom. My shoulders hunched beneath a painful weight, the contents of this room something to carry into the future.

A noise. Bubbling. Hissing.

Turning to the tub I kept my eyes on the tiled floor—white

tile, little woven dark blue rugs in front of the sink and the tub. Blue towels to match. The toilet. The shower curtain pulled aside.

Something in the tub.

Onyx jumped up, landing on the edge, walking along it delicately, inspecting. He meowed and I sagged, knees shaking. He looked from me to the tub and back, back and forth between myself and what lay in the tub.

Red. Deep and rich, vibrant and dark. It reminded me of split lips and open wounds, a dark splash on pavement, a smear on a severed ear. I sucked in a breath, another, fighting to keep my lungs full, sweat prickling in my armpits.

Cats will bring you half--dead things to teach you to hunt. They see you as another cat. Except you're an idiot who hasn't figured out how to hunt for yourself. They bring mice covered in puncture wounds, small rabbits with cracked necks, birds with broken wings—still breathing, living, desperate to escape the predator, waiting for a chance that will never come.

The thing in the tub was alive too.

Thing. Did it have a name anymore? Greg.

Breath bubbled out, his mouth torn open, split, the pink flesh of the cheeks exposed. Mad eyes, not angry, but full of fear, whites showing, rolling toward the cat, the bubbling breath turning into a choking, retching sound. Puncture wounds on his shoulder and chest, his lower body twisted at an unnatural angle. One arm barely attached, the fingers on the other hand opening and closing on nothing.

No more fists, no more backhanded slaps.

No more, no more, no more.

It circled through me and all I felt was relief.

Onyx jumped down, coming toward me, looking up to see what I thought. *Are you pleased?* Behind him, Greg's mouth was moving, a bloody hole, missing teeth, fighting to come together, to form words, to scream, to make any other sound than that hissing, bubbling tortured breathing.

I couldn't go any closer. I couldn't turn back. Call for help. *Call for help.* My cell phone was in my bedroom, forgotten along with the pile of clothes, beyond these walls there were other people, someone who would help Greg.

But.

What would I tell them? How would I explain my face? The bloody ex-boyfriend in my tub? There would be questions, faces pinched tight around suspicion, minds made up, decisions made. I would get one phone call. But I had no one to call.

The air in the room shifted, moving as something expanded, taking up space. The thing in the tub made a sound it hadn't before. Almost a yelp, louder than anything else so far. If it could have moved it would have, even now, it seemed to vibrate against the porcelain and I had to look away.

A large hand came to rest on my shoulder, gentle, the soft prick of claws resting against my flesh. There was height and muscle at my back, warmth and something like security, like safety. He breathed out, ruffling my hair, the scent of copper coming with it, fresh blood.

A muscled forearm came into view, covered in fine black fur, knobby fingers tipped with long black claws so sharp they cut the air as he pointed toward the tub. I turned slightly to see a shoulder covered in the same fur, the bulk of a dark body, a sharp face. He. But he turned me back, away from him—away from the monster that lived under my bed, the cat that followed me to the kitchen each morning for a can of smelly cat food. He urged me toward the tub, his chest to my back, with me as I took a stumbling step.

Look what I brought you.

I began to tremble, bile rising in my throat. I shook my head, a noise I didn't recognize coming from me. The thing in the tub gurgled, focused on the huge dark figure behind me, touching me. I was urged forward again, shown my meal, expected to eat. To finish what had been started.

"No," I said softly, shaking my head.

He made a noise, a question, so like the *merp* in the hall.

"I can't."

Let me.

I nodded. *Yes.* Yes, I would let him take care of it. I closed my eyes, squeezing them so tight, my face scrunched, keeping it all out. He turned me toward the door, guiding me through it, pushing me into the dim hall, sending me stumbling toward my room.

Behind me. Behind me were noises.

The air conditioner came on, cool air touching me, ruffling my hair as I passed beneath a vent in the hall. Evening light came to me from the bedroom, the curtains pulled back, gold and pink waiting to engulf me. Take me in. Give me something warm after the fluorescent glare of the bathroom; bare tile, wide eyes, deep red arterial blood. Heart's blood.

I lay down on my bed, on top of the quilt in various shades of green, rolling onto my side to face the window and watch the setting sun; knees up, arms curled in. The sounds from the bathroom continuing, going on until I thought they'd never stop, that I would live the rest of my life with those noises in my head. Wet chewing. The snap of a bone, cracking, marrow slurped. Then quieting, fading.

The bathroom door opened and I closed my eyes, squeezing them tight, refusing even to see the black world on the other side of my eyelids. I kept them closed as the air in the room changed, holding my breath as the bed dipped behind me, taking on weight. He fit himself to me, chest to back, knees tucked up with mine, arm coming over to take my hand, engulfing me.

Onyx began to purr.

The Body Snatchers

Marnie Vinge

Molly Southard sat in the very same examining room where she'd been diagnosed with a rare genetic condition as a child. Double organs, meaning she had an extra spleen. Now her own child was sitting on the exam table and the same pediatrician—now grayer and older—put two images on the light table mounted to the wall.

Dr. Parsons flipped the switch, illuminating the two images. MRI scans that they'd just gotten back on Alex, now thirteen, and having lived with the same rare genetic disorder as her mother her entire life.

"Looks about the way you described it, Molly," Dr. Parsons said, turning and clapping his hands together as if silently adding, *And that's that.*

At least there was no bad news. Molly felt her body begin to relax out of the grip her current emotional state kept her in most days at the moment. Just knowing that Alex was fine was a relief. Even if their lives were imploding all around them.

"How many of your patients have this kind of…thing?" Alex asked, her feet still dangling from the edge of the exam table, the paper sheet beneath her crinkling quietly with each movement of her legs.

Dr. Parsons cleared his throat.

Molly remembered asking the same question herself when she was a little girl on the brink of adolescence. She couldn't remember the answer, mostly because Dr. Parsons hadn't given it to her straight. He was more concerned with making her feel special rather than weird, and apparently citing statistics didn't cut it on that front for him. Molly knew it was rare, but she didn't know the percentage. She'd guess less than one.

"Well," Dr. Parsons looked nervously at Molly.

Though his bedside manner was impeccable, his straight-forwardness left something to be desired. Likely the price Molly and Alex were paying for the bedside manner. It irritated Molly as a kid and it irritated her now. It had made her feel weak. Like Dr. Parsons thought a kid couldn't handle the truth.

Molly gave him a nod. Alex was tough. She wasn't concerned about being weird. She was more concerned with surviving her parents' ugly divorce. The statistics on a non-fatal genetic condition were nothing to this kid, Molly thought and smirked to herself. Dr. Parsons turned to Alex, laying a hand gently on her shoulder. Alex's main interests and concerns lay with the paranormal ever since her parents split. Just before they left for Oklahoma, Alex's father had bought her all the ghost hunting paraphernalia she could ever want. She'd watched some reality TV shows about it and Molly was sure Mark had poured money onto the divorce wound in hopes that he'd be the fun parent. And it was likely Alex would get over this obsession just like many teenagers do.

"It's very rare. Maybe one in one-hundred thousand," he said. "But as I'm sure you've known, because of your mother, there's little to worry about. You just have an extra spleen. That's all," he concluded with a confirming pat on the shoulder and a warm smile.

"All is well," Dr. Parsons said. "So I take it that doing the checkup here means you've moved back?" As he asked the question, he sat down on his stool with a groan and a sigh, more evidence of how much time had passed since Molly had been back in her hometown.

"You would be correct," she said tersely, hoping her tone would serve as the opposite of an invitation to further questioning.

But Dr. Parsons didn't seem to pick up on it.

"You and Mark back in town," he remarked with a smile. The name cut Molly to the quick. She inhaled sharply, sucker-punched by the combination of consonants and vowels, and Dr. Parsons glanced at her as he made notes in Alex's chart.

At least she had a good poker face, Molly thought.

Dr. Parsons plowed on, undeterred.

"You two were high school sweethearts, right?" he asked.

"We were," she said. "Alex, why don't you get your backpack? I think Dr. Parsons probably has a whole bunch of other kiddos to get to today," she offered a smile to her daughter. It was so false, it felt like her cheeks might shatter.

It pained her, the expression on Alex's face. Molly knew that Alex knew her mother was hurting but the two of them didn't speak of it. It cast a pall over everything between them. There was no screaming, no yelling, but the silence was somehow worse. This make-believe of *Everything is fine. We're fine. Nothing needs to be talked about.*

It was in these moments—recognizing the shift in their relationship—that Molly thought about how, when Alex was little, she would sit in Molly's lap, tracing a heart into her palm. She'd fall asleep doing it. Sometimes so many times, that after she lost consciousness, Molly would have to rub her palm because it felt raw from the drawings of a little girl's sharp fingernail. That was a different time, though.

Now, it was like they lived in a minefield.

They'd tread across the eggshell charade so much, Molly wondered how much longer it could last.

Alex hopped up from the table and grabbed her pink backpack next to it.

Molly stood.

She pushed Alex gently toward the door and opened it for her.

"Go ahead and head out to the lobby," she whispered to her daughter and gave her what she hoped was an affirming squeeze of the arm. Alex looked at her and only nodded, having grown rather astute at determining the moments that were for adult conversation over the last six months.

Once she was out of earshot, Molly turned to Dr. Parsons.

"We're getting a divorce," she said and offered him an awkward smile, as if to lessen the blow for him even though it was her own cruel burden.

This was the part of returning home that she'd dreaded on the drive south. Everyone had known them: Molly and Mark, Mark and Molly. Proper nouns arranged based on which of them the person knew first. But this was where what remained of Molly's support system was. Her mother, with whom she and Alex were staying.

Any friends she might get back in touch with would likely meet her with a frostiness she didn't feel like dealing with. Not now at least.

"Oh, Molly," Dr. Parsons said. His face dropped, his features seeming sadder even now because of his age. The disappointment in his voice stung. It felt like blame even though Molly was sure he didn't intend for it to. Maybe that was projection, as the therapist she'd seen back in Omaha had told her.

A fat lot of good that had done them.

He seemed incredibly struck by this realization. As if it mattered to him.

"So it's just…the two of you?" he asked, almost like he was defusing a bomb or relaying the information to Molly for the first time.

"Yes. And Mom of course. It's alright," she assured him, immediately reminded of the way she cleaned up any emotional mess for Mark. Sanitized the dirty bits to keep him from feeling the intense pain that she did. But she wasn't sure that Mark shared any of that at any point. She wasn't sure he was capable of empathy anymore.

"Are you alright, though?" Dr. Parsons asked, raising an eyebrow.

"As alright as I can be, I suppose," she shrugged, but glanced toward the open doorway, thinking that her primary concern was if Alex would be okay.

"You will be," Dr. Parsons said. "One of these days, the pain will be gone. Like something from another life." His eyes drifted as he spoke, his tone almost dreamy.

Molly doubted this but thanked him for his sage advice and went out to the lobby where she found Alex locked in a staring contest with a clownfish inside the aquarium that had been there since Molly was a kid. A morbid thought came to Molly—how many fish had lived and died in that tank? Where in their number was the clownfish her daughter stared at?

Alex, lost in her thoughts with the fish, didn't notice her mother come out of the exam room. Just as well, Molly thought. It spared them from another stilted interaction. Jesus Christ, she had to get this under control.

Mark could leave her for someone younger, prettier, better in bed, but she'd be damned if he came between her and her daughter.

She went to the receptionist's desk just as Dr. Parsons popped out of the exam room and slipped into the booth behind the girl manning the phones.

"Hannah," he said to the girl, catching her attention.

He leaned down, pointed at something written on Alex's chart in illegible doctor scrawl, and Hannah nodded, following his finger along the page. He looked up and gave Molly a smile.

"Take care," he said.

She nodded, her social meter completely maxed out at this point. She wanted to go home and crawl into a bottle of sparkling wine and never come back out.

"Are you done?" Alex asked, coming up behind her. There was a note of exasperation in her voice that seemingly only belonged to teenagers. Molly smirked, then quickly wiped it from her face. She was glad for Alex to feel good enough to give her some attitude.

At least that felt semi-normal. And monumental, in a way.

She could deal with the attitude and the rolling eyes and the *but Mom*'s. She couldn't cope with the weird invisible curtain that seemed to have fallen between the two of them.

The receptionist, Hannah, took Molly's debit card as she offered it. Then she stood.

"I just need to make a phone call real quick," she told Molly. But she looked down, away from the woman whose payment she'd just taken. Molly watched as she turned away and dialed a number on the office phone. She murmured something into the receiver in tones too low for Molly to understand.

"Mom, can we get pizza for dinner?" Alex derailed any concentration Molly had left.

"Sure," she said, unable to take her eyes from the receptionist. Hannah was a young girl—maybe in college—with a brown ponytail looped into a makeshift bun. She wore a pair of purple scrubs and a sporty, periwinkle headband. She looked both confused and concerned as she got off the phone.

"Sorry about that," she said, once again averting her eyes from Molly.

Then something struck her. It should have been the first thing on her mind. This girl was young enough to be someone's little sister. Maybe someone that she and Mark had known back in the old days.

Molly wondered how much fodder her misfortune was providing the rumor mill in town.

The girl ran her card quickly and handed it back to Molly.

Molly took it a little too forcefully and shot the girl a sharp look.

"Here's your receipt," the girl handed her a piece of paper printed from the card reader. "And sign this one," she handed her their copy.

Molly scribbled quickly, pressing the pen a little too hard against the paper resting on the counter. It slipped making the '*d*' in Southard gain a long, angry, upward-sweeping tail. Molly slammed the pen onto the counter and offered the girl a smile that Molly was certain looked like it had been pressed out of her with a vise.

The girl gave her the same sheepish look she had earlier, almost like she found Molly intimidating. It gave Molly a strange sense of satisfaction, that look. It was the first time that the way someone had looked at her that gave Molly some sense of empowerment. Like maybe she wasn't a victim of her circumstances. She and Mark were on the verge of an agreement with the divorce. Her lawyer was waiting to hear from his. This seemed like a sign. Maybe things would go her way.

"Let's go," she placed a hand on Alex's shoulder and offered her a smile that was one of the few genuine smiles Molly had experienced in about six months. Alex smiled back at her, echoing the expression. And Molly almost swore *that* was genuine, too.

She didn't ask after its veracity, though. She didn't comment either.

She didn't want to jinx it.

———

"YOU WANNA SIT UP FRONT?" Molly asked Alex as they approached the back of the new-to-them Honda Civic. She glanced at the car, reminding herself that she shouldn't resent the fact that her entire life got turned upside down, because, for now at least, she had her daughter.

But it was hard. Every time she looked at the Honda, it served as a reminder of all that she'd already lost—and all she had yet to lose.

"Yeah," Alex said with a tiny hint of a smile that temporarily washed away Molly's financial worries. The pair of them got into the car and Molly turned the ignition. The Honda sputtered to life and she backed out as Alex buckled her seatbelt.

Molly pulled out onto Broadway—a smaller Broadway than she was used to back in Omaha—and turned right. Midday October, the street was less busy than after five, but a few cars dotted the lanes, passing Molly going in the opposite direction. Another car, a fine classic black Cadillac, passed them on the left and pulled ahead.

"Nice car," Molly murmured.

She tried to keep any note of bitterness locked tightly in her chest, not wanting Alex to take on any more of the emotional upheaval of their change in lifestyle than absolutely necessary.

"It looks like the kind of car a villain in a movie drives," Alex noted aloud, sitting forward in her seat to get a good look at it.

Molly turned on some music—a radio station, she wasn't sure which—and let it provide a little bit of ambient noise for the pair of them. Going up against silence was easier with a little FM help. A song came on, one that Molly remembered from high school. Alex seemed unphased, not knowing the words or the melody, and it made Molly sad.

Not because her daughter didn't know the song, but because it signaled the passage of time that had occurred since she'd left her hometown. The memories she associated with it were inaccessible to Alex, not hers at all. Memories of Mark and Molly when things were still good—when they were *amazing*.

Molly changed the station.

As they passed by many of the old businesses that Molly remembered, she took note of the way that things had changed, too.

Many of the signs and marquees were familiar. A general store here, a pharmacy there, a liquor store on the right, and a church on the left. The standard arrangement in the Bible Belt.

But as they got further from the center of town, new businesses seemed to have sprung to life in Molly's absence. In the corridor that used to have nothing but a field, there was now a strip mall. One on each side of the road, in fact.

The Cadillac that had pulled ahead switched lanes, getting in front of Molly.

She glanced at Alex, who seemed content, and that was about as much as Molly could ask for the time being.

Something caught her eye.

A giant marijuana leaf, bright green, over the entrance to a shop in one of the strip malls. Molly craned her neck, doing a double take, and turning long enough to get a solid look, proving to herself that she wasn't imagining things.

She'd known medical marijuana had passed in her home state during her absence. But to see a dispensary right there on the side of the road when she wouldn't have known who to talk to in order to buy weed during her formative years was a surreal sight.

And that's when it happened.

That brief moment put Molly and Alex on a collision course with destiny. It was like everything that had brought them here came to a head, coalescing in a few seconds in a way that neither of them would be aware of for a week.

"Mom!" Alex shouted, grabbing Molly's attention back just long enough for her to watch the Civic plow into the back of the black Cadillac.

The impact was sharp, jolting. More sudden than Molly could have imagined. The Cadillac had apparently slammed on its brakes, and before Molly could turn around to do the same, she'd rammed the nose of the Civic into the Cadillac going about thirty-five miles-per-hour.

The impact slammed Molly's forehead into the steering wheel. Alex jerked forward. Before Molly had time to look at her own injury, she turned to her daughter.

"Are you hurt? Are you alright?" Panic seized the breath from her chest as she blurted out the two conflicting questions.

Alex only nodded, her seat belt tightened across her body by the impact. She looked alright. Molly glanced in the rearview mirror and saw the great, reddening bruise that was beginning to form between her eyebrows and her hairline. A perfect, if somewhat exaggerated, impression of the curved arc of the steering wheel.

Then she looked out the windshield, steeling herself for whatever damage might meet her.

The hood of the Honda was crumpled, but not beyond its ability to drive—at least all the way to a car shop. The back of the Cadillac was dented, but the car seemed to be in way better shape than Molly's. She breathed a sigh of relief at that.

A knock at the driver's side window of the Honda made her jump out of her skin, still reeling from the adrenaline rush of the accident and the fevered panic of checking on Alex to make sure she was okay.

A woman stood there band waved. She smiled at Molly and looked past her at Alex. Her lips, painted candy apple red, pulled back to reveal two perfect rows of white teeth as she bent slightly at the waist to put her face even with Molly's.

Molly rolled the window down, listening to the groan of

the aging car's automatic window mechanism. It seemed like it was on its last leg, that this would be the final time it sunk into the door that might now be its grave.

It seemed fitting.

"Hi," the woman said brightly. "Are you guys alright?"

"We're fine. Are you okay?" Molly said quickly, her voice tight, still nervous about the whole situation. The afternoon that had been looking up turned around quickly in that split second Molly had taken to stare at the weed shop.

The woman seemed to focus less on Molly and more on Alex.

"How old are you?" she asked.

The question seemed probing and strange, coming out of nowhere, even though in any other circumstance it might have seemed quite normal.

Alex looked at Molly, and she nodded to her daughter.

Alex looked back at the woman at the window.

"Thirteen," she said.

"That's a fun age, huh, Mom?" Now the woman jostled Molly's arm inside the car, reaching across the invisible boundary between them. She gave her a wink, as if she understood the nightmare of raising a teenager. Molly relaxed slightly. She forced a laugh.

The woman's presence was warm. And she looked familiar somehow. Molly couldn't place her, though.

"I'm glad you're alright," the woman said to Molly and Alex. "I'm Melanie," she offered a hand to Molly.

Molly took it gingerly, still fully aware that the reason they were meeting now was because Molly had rear-ended the woman in her expensive car. And no matter how nice she was, it was unlikely that she'd be nice enough to forget about the whole thing.

"Molly," Molly said. "This is Alex," she gestured to her daughter who gave a small, timid wave. "I guess we need to call the police," Molly offered.

"*Pffffft,*" the woman threw her hands up as she made the noise of dismissal. "Look," she said, seriously then. "You're Molly Mercury, aren't you?" she asked. Her pupils seemed to dilate, as if the woman was taking in as much of Molly as she could.

Molly hadn't heard anyone use her maiden name in some time. It felt like a door thrown open in a stuffy room, allowing a breeze to rush through for the first time in years.

"I am," she said with a small smile. It felt good to be called that, better than Molly could have imagined. To be separate from Mark for once in her life—in this town—felt amazing.

"We went to high school together," Melanie said.

Molly felt a burst of shame color her cheeks and collarbone. She didn't instantly remember the woman. She wondered if it was age or perhaps just the trauma of her divorce coupled with the jarring accident moments prior. The woman seemed completely unshaken.

"I heard about what's going on with your ex," she said. "You know how people talk." She made another dismissive gesture as if she knew about that firsthand herself. She gave a dark chuckle with it, too. It was something that made Molly feel even more comfortable in her presence. The laugh wasn't fake. The gesture could have been. But the laugh was real. That gallows humor only certain people knew intimately.

"Let me take care of the car for you," Melanie said.

"I can't let you do that," Molly felt another burst of shame. Did her situation seem so dire to even outsiders that they felt the need to take pity on her? Anger flashed through her for a brief second. Then despair, pinning the anger down helplessly. She was in a position where the kindness of strangers might be her only refuge on some days. At least for now.

"You can, and you will," Melanie said simply. "That car is a tank," she pointed at the Cadillac. "Been in my family for a long time now. Been in lots of fender benders and none the worse for wear. They just don't make cars the way they used to, do they?" Melanie sighed with contentment, gazing at the old black vehicle.

She looked back at Molly.

"Let me pay to get yours fixed," she said again, this time more firmly. Less of an offer and more of a demand.

"I—"

"Tell you what," Melanie interrupted. "You can pay me back, but not in cash."

She glanced at Alex.

"I would imagine you're looking for some new friends, huh?" Melanie asked Alex.

Alex said nothing and Molly didn't force her to speak.

"The biggest favor you could do for me is let your daughter come to a party my daughter is having this Friday night," she said. "My daughter doesn't have a lot of friends, and God knows she needs some. It's her birthday," she added under her breath. She looked at Alex. "And I imagine you might be in need of some, too."

Molly looked at Alex. Her expression had softened as she warmed to the idea.

"Okay," Molly found herself saying after Alex gave her a small smile. These would probably be the kids Alex would be joining in school as soon as Molly got her enrolled. It would be good for both of them. Molly could seize the evening as an opportunity to spend some much needed alone time. And Alex might not spend her entire night either on her Nintendo Switch or on YouTube, looking for videos of real ghosts.

"What time and where?" Molly asked, her tone brightening. Maybe things were actually going to turn out alright anyway.

"You know the house," Melanie said with a smirk. "Top of the hill over there," she pointed behind them. Molly turned to look, but the strip mall obscured her view. "And if you, by some stroke of luck, don't know the house from the inside, you definitely know it from the outside."

Molly looked back at Melanie.

"McMasters," she said with a grin, bearing those perfect teeth once more.

She handed Molly a business card that she seemed to produce with sleight of hand.

Molly took the card, staring at the business name emblazoned in black ink on a lovely off-white linen-textured card. Molly knew instantly why the name sounded familiar. Melanie walked away.

Melanie McMasters lived in the most famous house in Molly's hometown.

The McMasters Funeral Home.

Molly remembered Melanie now.

And her stomach sank.

———

"HELP ME BRING THE GROCERIES IN," Molly told Alex as they pulled into the driveway of Molly's parents' home. A house that they'd lived in for the entirety of Molly's life. Her father had died in this house. Now, only her mother—Alex's grandmother—remained as its sole inhabitant before Molly had called to tell her about the divorce.

"Okay," Alex grumbled.

It was another sign of normalcy that made Molly feel better in a strange way.

Molly kept picking away at the interaction with Melanie McMasters earlier. The memories that surrounded it were messy.

The two of them took the groceries in—bought on their way home from the fender bender—and though the Honda looked rough, it was drivable.

Molly fumbled for her keys, but as they approached the front porch, her mother flung the screen door open.

"There are my girls," she said warmly.

It hurt Molly's heart how much her mom seemed to enjoy having them here. Alex wasn't quite as close to her as she should be, Molly knew. She and Mark had moved to Omaha for his job. The distance had worn on any connection Alex might have had with either set of grandparents. But Molly imagined that maybe this would provide their daughter with an opportunity to foster this relationship, at least. The only remaining one she had with a grandparent.

"Hi," Alex said quietly.

"Hi, Mom," Molly leaned in and gave her mom a kiss on the cheek as she passed into the house.

The three of them made short work of putting things away. Then Dolores, Molly's mother, took her seat in her favorite chair in the living room. Alex ran to her bedroom and grabbed her Nintendo Switch, returning a moment later and planting herself on the far side of the couch. Molly sat on the opposite end, giving her teenage daughter some space, grateful that she'd chosen to play her game in here rather than slink away to her bedroom to mope away the evening.

"I ran into somebody from high school today," Molly said as her mother changed the TV channel, opting for local news.

"Not hard to do around here," Dolores said.

"She literally ran into her," Alex offered.

Dolores looked at the two of them.

"Did you not see the car, grandma?" Alex asked.

Dolores raised her eyebrows and looked at Molly.

"We had a little fender bender. It's fine," Molly assured her mother. She gave her a look and her mother asked no further questions. Molly had told her she was exhausted from answering them. "Anyway, I ran into the McMasters girl. The one I went to high school with."

"From the funeral home?" Dolores asked.

Molly nodded.

"I'm letting Alex go to a slumber party there this week-end," she added.

Alex said nothing, now focused on her Switch.

Dolores laughed, almost to herself.

"You remember how scared you kids were of that place?" she asked. "Every single one of you girls were scared of Melanie McMasters. And all the rumors. Stories going back to when your daddy and I met almost fifty years ago."

Alex seemed to perk up her ears, looking from her grand-mother to her mother.

"Just stories," Molly said to Alex. "Urban legends. All towns have one. Ours just happened to be *this*."

"What kind of rumors?" Alex asked, instantly in her wheelhouse, sensing a creepy story on the verge of telling.

"Oh, nothing," Molly said, dismissing it. But Dolores wasn't so quick to move on.

"Everyone thought that the McMasters were a family of witches back when your grandfather and I started dating. Way back in high school, the very high school your mama went to."

Molly gave Dolores a look, but Alex was sitting forward in her seat, the most engaged she'd been with her grandmother since they'd moved in.

"It was said that they were body snatchers, of a sort," Dolores went on. "That they would sometimes abduct people and use their bodies for experiments. Trying to become immortal."

"Like vampires?" Alex asked.

"Not exactly," Dolores went on. "More like Victor Frankenstein, I think."

Alex nodded solemnly. She'd read the famous Mary Shelley novel a year prior.

"Every so often, someone would go missing and the stories would start up again. It wasn't very often. But all it took was one missing person to fire up the rumor mill again."

Alex glanced at Molly.

"*Rumors*," Molly emphasized.

"But grandma said you were scared of them," Alex interjected.

"Well, I was a teenager," Molly said.

"I'm a teenager," Alex replied.

"And quite a brave one to go spend the night there," Dolores smirked. Alex gave her a smile.

"Braver than me at your age, I'm afraid," Molly said.

"Did you ever get invited over there?" Alex asked.

"I think it's time for you to play on your Switch," Molly said with a forced smile, then shot her mother a look saying that the conversation was definitely over.

———

AS THE WEEK WORE ON, Molly found herself thinking more and more about high school. She went back to her conversation with Melanie McMasters. The moment when she realized who the woman was—what their connection had been—and how she hadn't even remembered her at first.

She wondered if Melanie still thought about her.

That day after gym class when they'd stolen her clothes. Hid them from her. Called her a freak and a witch. A kid had gone missing a few weeks prior—just around the corner from Halloween and Melanie's father had been in poor health—and once again the stories about the McMasters family and their business fired up like clockwork. The kid was found, her father died shortly thereafter. The memory, looked at through the cold lens of adulthood was haunting.

The group of girls that Molly had hung out with in high school were popular. Molly was popular. She and Mark were prom king and queen their senior year.

Melanie McMasters was an outsider to all of that. She was a typical goth kid. Wore black, dramatic makeup, listened to The Cure too loud as she whipped out of the parking lot on a Friday afternoon. None of those things would so much as raise an eyebrow in a metropolitan area, but in their small town it definitely helped to magnify the target on Melanie's back when they were younger.

All of those girls that Molly had been friends with had left their small town. Just like she had.

But now she was back.

She needed to apologize to Melanie. It was as simple as that.

When Friday arrived, Molly stared into the mirror of her single sink bathroom after washing her face. She patted her skin dry and applied moisturizer, taking note of every little rusted spot on the glass in front of her.

The house she'd shared with Mark in Omaha was beautiful. And well beyond her solitary means now. Mark was still living there, along with a woman who would surely become his second wife. Molly thought bitterly about how she probably had all of her things arranged on the counter the way that Molly once had.

Molly threw on some makeup, hoping that she could make herself look at least slightly presentable if she was going to apologize to Melanie before she dropped Alex off.

Over the course of the week, Melanie had arranged for a rental car for them while the Honda was repaired.

"Are you ready?" Molly called out to Alex, just across the hall.

"Just a second!" Alex called back from her bedroom. The sound traveled easily in Dolores' small house.

She glanced at herself in the mirror one more time, telling herself eventually she was going to have to start thinking in terms of *now*. Her new life. No matter how badly she wanted her old one back.

But she wasn't quite there yet.

She left the bedroom and went across the hall, leaning, arms crossed, against her daughter's open doorway.

Alex scrambled to place different things in her bag as if she were packing for a trip to Everest, not just an overnight stay down the street.

"You're not even going to be gone twenty-four hours," Molly said with a small laugh. "And you'd better not be taking any of your *equipment* with you."

Alex shot her a fiery glare and Molly held up her hands and shut her mouth, not wanting a fight, especially if some defiance meant Alex was doing better. It was one of the first displays of real anger Alex had shown her.

Something the therapist might have said was progress.

"Okay, I'm ready," Alex said after zipping her bag tight, the contents making it almost burst at the seams. But Molly didn't dare tell her the straps might break or something might come unstitched. Instead, she just led the way to the car.

"I'll be back, mom," Molly called to her mother.

Dolores waved at Alex and wished her a happy sleepover.

"And don't let any body snatchers get you!" She laughed as the pair of them went out the front door.

Dark had already fallen, mid-October in the Southwest had always been Molly's favorite season. She had loved the early nights, the crisp chill in the air, the omnipresent Halloween decor.

But this year was different.

Molly found the early fall of darkness isolating, symbolic of her current circumstance. The chill in the evening air was cutting her to the bone. It felt like it had penetrated the leather jacket she wore and was biting at her skin. Like nothing could warm her up ever again. The festivities surrounding the impending holiday felt hollow. It would be a performance, whatever they decided to do for Alex this year. An attempt at new traditions when that was the last thing Molly wanted to be building.

Alex put her earbuds in on the way, turning her music up loud enough that Molly could hear the lyrics clearly over the sound of the rental car's engine. It was far nicer than the old Civic. She snuck a glance at Alex at the stoplight, watching how the headlights of turning cars cast a ghostly white light across her daughter's face.

And that brought her back to all the talk surrounding the McMasters house. And her upcoming apology to Melanie.

Molly lost herself in those memories long enough for her and Alex to make it to the hill on the edge of town where the McMasters Funeral Home had rested for almost a century. Molly pulled into the circular driveway, under the awning that led to the ancient porch on the front side of the house. Two hearses were parked silently on the side of the house, where bodies were brought out—and in —presumably.

Molly knew the latter for certain. McMasters had buried her father.

The porch glowed orange, courtesy of ancient sconces on either side of the double doors.

"You ready?" she asked Alex.

She was really asking herself that very question.

Alex stared out the passenger side window, then looked back at her mother.

She gave a silent nod with a smile that made Molly almost cancel the whole thing. Alex's smile faded and she chewed gently on her bottom lip, her slightly crooked front teeth showing. Teeth that Molly and Mark were going to have an orthodontist look at after Christmas. That was before everything.

A sadness washed over Molly. And it was followed quickly by resolve. Alex was going to this party. She was going to make friends.

"You can do this," Molly said.

Alex nodded, smiling a little more this time. Molly wished

her own words were of any comfort to herself. But they weren't. Alex was brave though. Far braver than her mother.

Alex and Molly got out of the car and just as both doors shut, Molly saw Melanie McMasters appear at the door, a halo of orange heralding her arrival.

———

"THERE YOU TWO ARE!" Melanie called from the doorway. One of the double doors yawned outward, red light from inside bathing the porch in flames.

"Party lights?" Molly asked as they approached. Alex seemed to hang back slightly.

"You know it," Melanie answered with a slight laugh. "Alex, are you ready to meet Sylvia?"

Alex looked at her mother.

It occurred to Molly that up until this moment, she hadn't known Melanie's daughter's name. She nodded at Alex, who nodded—albeit less forcefully—at Melanie.

"Well, let's go," Melanie said with a bright flash of those perfect teeth.

She ushered the two of them inside. The entry hall was coated in red, giving the place a more ominous feel than Molly remembered from her dad's funeral just months before Alex was born. Alex had already been here, in the protection of her mother's womb. It felt like a metaphor for the divorce. Alex was facing life now *sans* protection. Molly wasn't sure there was any way that she could offer it to her daughter now.

The entry hall was as Molly remembered. Carpeted with doorways off to the left and right down a long hallway. Each of those led to a state room. One to an arrangement office. Out of sight, perhaps in the basement was the prep room.

The place where they prepared the bodies.

Where they had prepared her father's body.

Perhaps it was fitting that one of the first actions Molly

and Alex were taking towards building a new life was happening in a place that dealt in death and grief.

"The birthday girl is right in there," Melanie gave Alex a gentle guiding push toward a state room just down the hall where music seemed to be emanating from. Molly could make out laughter as well.

Alex disappeared into the room and Molly turned her focus on mending things with Melanie.

"Melanie," she said.

Melanie turned to look at her.

"I know what you're going to say," Melanie told her. Her tone was gentle yet abrupt. She held up a hand. "You don't need to apologize for things way back then," she offered a smile. "It was a long time ago, we're all different people now."

Molly was taken aback.

"Besides, you letting Alex come over here tonight is far more than any apology could ever do," her tone was serious, carrying some heaviness that Molly couldn't quite put her finger on. She shifted nervously from foot to foot.

"Besides," Melanie said. "I know you got made fun of plenty in grade school. What with the extra…" she pointed to Molly's stomach.

The gesture felt invasive. Molly jerked back involuntarily. The way that Melanie pointed to her abdomen and spoke with such knowing unnerved Molly.

Kids had made fun of her in grade school after she came back after one summer where she'd gained an education on her extra spleen. They'd called her all sorts of names. Somehow that had faded in junior high. Molly had become someone else. She'd embraced the popular girls, doing and saying and acting however she needed to in order to make them love her.

If they loved her, everyone else would fear her.

She knew that, even at fourteen.

But just now, Melanie pointing out that one flaw

connected to a painful portion of her life, made her feel infinitely and uncomfortably vulnerable. It was an unwelcome penetration of a shield Molly thought was impeccable. Unbroachable by anyone now.

But apparently it wasn't.

Maybe it was that her defenses were weakened by the current state of her life. She wasn't sure. But she tried to shift gears.

"Thank you," she said. "I do need to apologize, though." Now, she cared less about the actual apology and more about putting the focus on something she could control. "I'm sorry for all of that."

Melanie waved it away like water under a very old bridge.

"Not to worry," Melanie said with a smile that seemed genuine.

Molly offered one of her own, though sadder than Melanie's.

"I guess I'll come back to get her around noon tomorrow?" Molly half-stated.

"That sounds perfect," Melanie said. "Gives us plenty of time."

Melanie ushered her to the door, her last statement hanging in the air between them. Molly thought it was odd. But as she got into her car, she reminded herself that there were things far more odd than that.

Such as how quickly her marriage had fallen apart.

And how she found herself driving to her childhood home.

Once she arrived, she sat in the driveway with the car off.

She cried for an hour and then went inside.

———

"THE BIRTHDAY GIRL is right in there," the McMasters woman said to Alex as she gave her a gentle but strong push towards a room down the hallway. Alex put one foot in front of the other, but glanced back at her mother one last time. She was already absorbed in conversation with Melanie.

Alex felt her teeth digging into her bottom lip to the point that, if she didn't quit soon, she'd draw blood. Some ghost hunter she made. Frightened at the very prospect of spending the night in a funeral home. She'd never make it if this is how scared she got before anything supernatural had even happened.

And she had no guarantee that it would.

Earlier, stuffing her bag full of odds and ends, items she'd gotten her dad to buy her that had to do with ghost hunting, she'd felt like she was about to embark on an adventure. Now, she felt silly and unequipped to deal with that adventure. She just wanted to go home.

As she looked back, she noticed once more how beautiful Melanie was. How peaceful her features seemed. She seemed younger than her age—the same as her mom—and next to Molly, Alex could see how tired her mom really was. How much the last few months had really worn her down. The pain was etched on her face in lines that Alex feared would become permanent.

It made Alex sad enough that she looked away and headed for the open doorway where music spilled out. And she immediately spotted the girl whose birthday it must be. Strangely, though, she was alone in the red-lit room. Party music played, but there weren't many festivities happening here.

Sylvia McMasters walked right up to her, the girl a miniature of her own mother. Just as beautiful and vibrant. A strange combination of traits for two people that had apparently lived in a funeral home all their lives.

It made Alex wonder how much truth there was to any of the rumors. They seemed like perfectly nice people. Maybe just maligned because of where they lived and worked. Sylvia greeted her with a wide, warm smile. Alex raised a hand to her own crooked teeth, covering them as she smiled and blushed at the girl.

"You must be the girl my mom told me about!" Sylvia said, her voice colored with enthusiasm.

Alex wondered how few friends she had. Why weren't any of them here?

Sylvia's presence was magnetic. Like a bug zapper during a dark summer night, drawing Alex nearer. She also felt a sense of trepidation in getting so close. Like Sylvia might strike unexpectedly. A beautiful viper like those Alex had seen on National Geographic documentaries.

It was an absurd image, likely fueled by the rumors she'd read online and the story her grandmother had told earlier in the week. As silly as it seemed, it gave her a falling sensation in her gut, like she'd crested the first hill of a rollercoaster and was about to experience the drop. It felt the way unwanted truths often do.

Alex brushed it off, echoing something her mother had told her one night the previous week.

It can be scary to start over. Even as an adult. And especially as a kid.

That's how this felt: scary.

As quickly as Sylvia had found herself interested in Alex, her attention drifted, flitting to a retro stereo from which the music must have been coming. She fiddled with the dials as Alex watched.

"How about something to drink?" Melanie's voice floated into the room from across the hall as she called to Alex. Sylvia was undisturbed.

Alex crept forward, her shoes shuffling against dark brown carpet that lined the entrance to the funeral home. She peered into the room just across the hallway. She spotted Melanie, sitting on a bench seat beneath a beautiful stained glass window.

The moonlight outside poured through the colored panes,

casting a dark ruby glow against Melanie's cheek as she looked at Alex. This room was not well-lit like the hallway and the other state room. In front of Melanie was a lengthy buffet table covered in sweets and decorations for the party. All of them remained untouched.

Alex took a step inside.

She nodded at Melanie, accepting her offer of something to drink.

Melanie smiled and stood from the window seat.

"Help yourself to anything on the table," she said.

Alex looked over the sweets, each looking more delectable than the last. She grabbed a chocolate covered strawberry and bit into it, the tart fruit bursting across her taste buds, wrapped in the velvety taste of milk chocolate.

Melanie reached for the long-handled ladle resting in a large bowl of red liquid. Punch, from the smell. Alex stepped closer and took the glass from Melanie. She brought it to her lips and sniffed it. Something sour seemed to lurk beneath the sickly sweet scent.

"Drink up," Melanie said. Her voice was lower, smoother. And she watched Alex with all the intensity of a predatory animal.

It made Alex uncomfortable but she did as she was told, remembering her mom telling her far too many times how rude it is to refuse food from someone when you're a guest in their home.

She swallowed the bitter drink and forced a smile.

Melanie returned it.

"Good?" she asked.

Alex nodded, perhaps too vigorously, but she hoped that Melanie wouldn't detect any dishonesty.

"Go ahead and finish that, then we'll get started," Melanie told her.

"Where is everyone else?" Alex asked.

"Everyone we need is already here," Melanie replied with a Sphinx-like smile.

Melanie's eyes never left Alex, but Alex found herself looking away, a little shy and embarrassed of the attention and almost feeling as if Melanie would watch her long enough to see her do something wrong. That she might realize Alex was hunting for ghosts tonight.

But she made no comment of the kind.

Alex gulped the punch, biting back the urge to make a bitter face as she drank the last. It reminded her of a time when she was a kid and accidentally took a drink of her father's beer.

She held the glass out to Melanie, and felt something funny happening in her head.

The glass began to shake and she was losing feeling in her arm. But Melanie just watched, her smile never faltering. Alex stumbled backwards, the glass in her hand tumbling down to the floor between them. The thick glass only bounced on the carpet below. The thud seemed muffled. Alex got dizzy. Her vision blurred. She reached for Melanie and felt herself falling.

And then everything went black.

———

A MONOTONOUS, rhythmic beep was the first thing Alex noticed as she regained consciousness.

Beep. Beep. Beep.

The sound was instantly familiar, though Alex had to struggle to know from where. Then it hit her—the time her mom was in the hospital, her ankle broken on a ski trip. It was the sound of a heart monitor.

She opened her eyes slowly to an almost blinding brightness directly above her. A sanitized cool white light shone down upon her. The kind of light you might find in a police station, or a hospital.

But there was something else about the room surrounding her. It stank of something unholy. Like death. Or what Alex imagined death to smell like. The funeral home. Preservatives. Formaldehyde.

Fuzzy figures moved about beside her. She still couldn't speak or move. And then a gloved hand placed a mask over her mouth and nose.

The figure of a man hovered near and began to come into focus. Alex's head pounded.

When he spoke, she recognized his voice. The rhythm of his speech boomed against her skull. The light intensified the headache tenfold.

"You're doing great, Alex," he said. "This will be over before you know it."

It was Dr. Parsons.

Then the world went black once more.

———

ALEX WOKE IN EXTRAORDINARY PAIN. She cried out and found her tongue stalled by fabric. A gag in her mouth with a rotten taste. The smell of it flooded her nostrils, making her woozy once more.

But the pain was so strong that her focus barely zeroed in on the smell of the rag. The neurons in her brain were sending a pain signal from her abdomen. She moved slightly upon waking, and a fresh wave of pain fired through her body, lighting her up like a Christmas tree. She bit down on the gag and saw white stars exploding behind her eyelids.

She felt that she might faint, but didn't.

Alex had never had surgery. But she injured her ankle during a soccer game once when she was nine years old. The pain had radiated as she healed the bad sprain, but this was something entirely apart.

This was far worse.

The wound felt deep, internal.

This was pain without the edges blunted. She was afraid to look at her stomach for fear of what kind of wound she might find there. Her heart rate sped up at the thought. She breathed rapidly, shallowly, through her nose, inhaling the tangy, metallic scent of blood.

There was something infinitely more disgusting about smelling blood than only tasting it. Alex thought about the time when she had bitten her lip so hard that she'd tasted it instantly. You can't smell a drop of blood. Not unless you're a shark.

The acrid scent drifting past her olfactory glands was coming from a lot more than a droplet. She kept her eyes closed, still smelling it, beginning to hear the sounds and voices around her. She wanted to stay in her own little world, her eyes squeezed shut protecting her from whatever reality lay beyond.

God, there must be so much.

After that thought came another.

The wound in her abdomen was deep. She could tell that.

There's so much and it's mine.

The last two words: *it's mine* were enough to make Alex feel like she might faint once more. She clenched her jaw around the gag, grinding her teeth into the cloth until she could almost feel the bone-on-bone contact of her upper and lower molars. And then she opened her eyes.

Everything came into focus slowly. The muffled sounds became louder, more clear. Voices, moaning, a gurgling sound that made Alex's stomach turn. Shapes and shadows, people, all twisting into focus like the subjects of a director's lens.

She was sitting at a dining table. The room lit only by taper candles in a candelabra on each end. Around the table sat Melanie, Sylvia, Dr. Parsons, a woman who seemed to be his wife, and the elderly person sitting directly across from her, barely able to keep their almost bald head upright.

Her eyes settled on the figure directly across from her.

She was a woman, though her ancient age made it almost hard to tell. Her hair had all but fallen out, like one might see on a corpse decomposing in the elements on some late-night forensic show. Her skin was cracked and worn, deep lines telling the story of her life. The hardships and the laughter marking her skin side by side. The woman looked so fragile that if someone suddenly blew out the candles, she might disintegrate into smoke along with the flames.

The woman sat in the chair, her head barely holding itself up. She stared at Alex with milky white eyes, giving her a ghastly appearance. Alex fought to keep her focus on the woman, willing herself not to pass out. The woman licked her dry lips with a tongue rigid as a reptile's.

"Eat, mother," Melanie said from her spot at the end of the table.

"How exactly does this work?" Dr. Parsons piped up from the end of the table. Alex looked at him, turning her head slowly and feeling as if she must be having a nightmare. His voice was tremulous, not holding the self-assurance it had when she was in his office earlier in the week.

Melanie shot the doctor a look, indicating now was not the time for questions. The woman beside him gripped his hand tightly. He gave her a reassuring look, but neither of them seemed comfortable with what was happening.

Then Alex looked back at the old woman's plate and felt vomit creep into the back of her throat, the bile burning her sinuses with nowhere else to go. The only pleasant thing was that the stench of her own innards triumphed over the scent of her own blood for a few moments.

On the plate was what appeared to be raw meat, bloody still.

Almost black with blood, it sat, plated finely on china. The blood on top of it dripped down either side like gravy atop a steak. The shape of the cut looked familiar to Alex but she couldn't place it immediately.

It took Alex a moment. The wound in her abdomen. The deep pulsating pain. The bloody yet familiar shape on the plate in front of the old woman.

Spleen.

Alex watched in horror.

"You have to eat it," Melanie prompted her mother again, this time less politely. "That's how it works, you know this."

The old woman sniffed the plated meal before her and turned up her nose. Alex swallowed down the last of the bile. Her sinuses still burned with the scent of digestion.

She glanced down again at Dr. Parsons and the woman beside him. This time she took in her appearance. She had a kerchief tied around her head. Her eyebrows were gone and she was gaunt. The two of them watched the old McMasters woman intently, with something Alex thought she could identify as hope.

"I'm so sorry," Melanie laughed nervously as she looked over at Dr. Parsons. "It's an unpleasant process for everyone involved." She went on then to answer his question. "We want her to consume the organ so that her soul can have a new host. The girl's soul will then find itself inside this body," she stroked her mother's cheek gently. "Then, your beautiful wife can have the…mother's." She glanced at Dr. Parsons. "Consuming one of the double organs means that the new host—in this instance, Alex—will continue to have a healthy body and the prospective soul or *virus*, if you will, will inhabit the new host. It's why when we came to our little arrangement, I told you we needed someone with a double organ. It didn't matter which."

Dr. Parsons said nothing, but when his eyes caught Alex's, he looked away quickly. Almost as if he were ashamed.

"Eat it," Melanie instructed her mother.

But the woman wouldn't. So Melanie stood from her chair and stabbed the thing on the plate with a fork. She grabbed her mother's knife roughly and began to saw. The organ split open, more blood pooling around it on the white china. Alex felt herself grow nauseated.

Melanie stabbed a piece—a large chunk—with her fork and put it up to her mother's mouth.

"Eat," she bit off the word sharply.

The woman shook her head, barely able to comprehend her daughter, her mind so gone.

Melanie grabbed her jaw like a dog's. She forced her mouth open. The old woman moaned and fought her with what little life force he had. She struggled.

"Help me!" Melanie shouted at Dr. Parsons.

He sat, bewildered for a moment, then rose to the occasion.

Together, they subdued the old woman. Dr. Parsons held her face straight forward, Melanie forced the spleen into her mouth one bloody bite after another. She gurgled on the blood, she gagged on the meat, vomiting once only for her daughter to shovel it all back into her mouth until the woman swallowed her own sick, too exhausted to fight anymore.

Bite by sickening bite, Alex listened to the sounds of cannibalism.

Her very own spleen, split wide open, being choked down someone's throat. The ache in her abdomen pierced her sharply, as if her remaining spleen felt sympathy pains for its twin being consumed only a few feet away.

Alex forced herself to watch. To bear witness to whatever this monstrosity was. The old woman gulped, forced to swallow unchewed pieces of the organ as its original host sat, bloody and aching across from her, a pound or two lighter.

Alex listened to the wet, sickening smack of the old woman's jaws coming together, gum against gum, doing her best to pulverize the chunks of Alex's organ, as blood dripped from her chin. She moaned, fighting her captors, but swallowing the organ just the same.

And finally, it was done.

The blood on the plate ran back together slowly after Melanie got her mother to swallow the last piece. She dropped the fork to the plate with a clang. The old woman was exhausted, and judging the looks on both Melanie and Dr. Parsons' faces, they were as well.

Alex felt herself grow woozy. Once more, something strange was happening inside of her. Though this time it wasn't just in her head. Her whole body was responding to something, like the call of a siren. She wondered if she was dying. She felt herself becoming very loosely tethered to reality, to her own body.

Melanie stood and walked over to Alex. She reached around to the back of her head, untied the gag, and gently tugged it from her mouth.

"Just a few minutes," Melanie breathed into her ear, reassuring her. Of what, Alex wasn't sure. Perhaps reassuring her that death would end all of this soon.

Alex inhaled deeply, feeling a serenity come over her. She closed her eyes.

"Thank you my dear," she heard a strangely familiar voice speaking. A voice she'd only ever heard played back to her over a cell phone video or a recording. "That extra spleen came in handy, didn't it?"

Her own voice.

There was laughter around the table. Almost a sense of relief.

Alex opened her eyes.

The scene in front of her was blurry, as if her vision was clouded from the center outward. Her whole body hurt, felt lifeless. She couldn't move. From the periphery she caught Melanie's hair. Across the table. Had she walked back over to her mother?

She could taste blood in her mouth. The gag was entirely gone.

She tried to move, but her body was too weak.

She tried to speak and heard only the moans of the old woman reverberating out of her tired lungs and trachea.

What was happening?

Then without warning, Melanie was back at her side, speaking into her ear.

"Thank you, Alex," she whispered.

Alex tried to speak once more, but couldn't.

"Your sacrifice means more to us than you know," she went on.

Finally Alex rasped out one word.

"Why?"

She clutched at Melanie's arm with all her strength, her new, bony fingers digging into the woman's flesh beside her.

"So we can live forever, of course," Melanie said and then directed a small laugh toward everyone else in the room. Then she focused back on Alex. Out of the corner of her eye, she thought she saw Melanie's smile. She spoke once more.

"It's the family tradition, my dear. My father wasn't so lucky. We thought the boy we took had a similar anatomy to your own, but it turned out not to be true. And we didn't work quickly enough to get your mother back then."

She stroked Alex's nearly bald scalp as realization began to truly dawn on the girl.

The rumors. The urban legend.

Body snatchers.

A vague remembrance of a sentiment her grandmother might have expressed while telling the story.

Every once in a while someone would go missing.

Alex felt herself begin to breathe heavily.

It was real.

———

HANNAH WATCHED Dr. Parsons and Melanie McMasters restrain the old woman—the McMasters matriarch—as they force fed her the organ belonging to the little girl sitting across the table from her. At one point, Dr. Parsons' wife turned her face away and almost spotted Hannah.

Hannah slid down the brick facade of the house, her heart pounding in her chest. It thundered in her ears. Her vision tunneled.

This was worse than she suspected. This was insane.

This was the urban legend come to life.

Body snatchers, just as she'd been told in grade school. And she couldn't help but feel that she'd helped to make this come to pass. The notes on the chart. The call to the number she didn't recognize. It was all too much of a coincidence.

Hannah stayed, frozen to the spot for what seemed like a never-ending moment. She wasn't sure she could summon the courage to move.

But she had to.

She couldn't let this happen. Not to the girl she'd seen just a week ago.

She had to get to Alex Southard's mother.

They had to get Alex out of that house.

———

MOLLY SPENT the majority of the evening watching television with her mom. Dolores laughed at the jokes on her favorite sitcom. Molly wasn't sure she still had the ability to laugh at anything she watched or read. She was in that stage of grief where even escape, through media, was impossible. Her focus didn't last long enough and everything reminded her of the life she was leaving behind. Morning coffee with Mark on the patio off their bedroom. The inside jokes shared between her husband and her daughter. The feeling of being a family.

And her mind kept going back to Alex.

Leaving her at the party.

Had it been the right thing to do? She'd seemed nervous. Was Molly doing more to assuage her own guilt and avoid paying for a car repair than she was for Alex's well-being?

The thought made her want to vomit.

She sat up on the couch and grabbed her purse, still sitting at her feet.

"I'm going to go get Alex," she told her mother.

Dolores looked at her, puzzled.

"Are you worried about all those stories?" she asked her daughter.

"No, it's not that," Molly said. Though, if she was being honest with herself, there was a part of that that bothered her. Not that she thought there was much truth to it, but leaving her daughter with Melanie had been a mistake. She'd go pick her up and tell them she was sorry, but Alex needed to come home. She'd make something up. Maybe Dolores had to be taken to the hospital. Or Mark called—hah! That was a laugh. Mark hadn't called since Molly and Alex had left.

She would think of something believable. It didn't really matter.

She just wanted Alex safe at home with her.

"You should just let her stay, Molly," Dolores called out as Molly grabbed her coat and keys and unlocked the front door.

She paused for a moment, but said nothing, unwilling to argue about this with her mother. She wouldn't have been able to tell her why or what had prompted the train of thought that led her to this moment, but Molly knew that she wanted —*needed*—Alex to be at home with them.

Sooner rather than later.

She got into the car quickly, sealing out the bitter chill of an October midnight. She shifted the car into reverse, but as she did, a set of headlights came to a screeching halt just past the sidewalk in front of her mother's house. With the car still running, the driver exited the vehicle and rushed to Molly's window, slamming their fist against the glass.

"Get the fuck away from me!" Molly shouted at the person, unable to make out any of their features in the darkness.

"Mrs. Southard!" The girl in front of her threw back the hood of her hoodie and Molly recognized her. Hannah, from the clinic. Dr. Parsons' receptionist.

Hannah backed up but paced nervously, waiting for Molly to roll down her window.

"What's the matter?" Molly asked the girl, feeling uneasy about the whole thing.

"We have to go get your daughter," Hannah blurted out.

Molly felt a panic swell in her chest. It was the foreboding she'd felt earlier, but now it wasn't just an anxiety in the back of her mind that she couldn't trace to anything logical. Now, a stranger was telling her something was wrong.

Her heart raced.

"What's going on?" she demanded of the girl.

Her face in the moonlight was blanched, pale. Her eyes were wild, as if she'd seen a ghost.

"It's all true!" Hannah shrieked.

"Get in the car," Molly told her.

Hannah seemed to stand there, unable to move in one direction or the other.

"Hannah, get in the goddamned car *now*," Molly said with more authority than she'd ever said anything in her life. Not even when she told Mark their marriage was over. And he was fighting the divorce settlement with all he had, thanks to his new girlfriend.

Hannah nodded, seemingly in shock.

She rushed around to the passenger side and slid in, slamming the door.

Molly backed out of the driveway and peeled out in the rental car, the pair of them leaving Hannah's sedan running, parked in the street with the driver's side door wide open.

———

"I NEED you to tell me what's happening, Hannah," Molly said evenly as she floored it across town. Hannah sat, recovering from almost hyperventilating. Finally, she seemed like some of the shock of the evening had worn off, leaving her ready to debrief her driver.

"What do you mean, *it's all true?*" Molly asked.

Hannah stared forward and spoke, sounding like she'd spent the last five minutes recovering from a marathon.

"The rumors," she said. "The urban legend. You know the story, don't you?"

Molly felt a jolt in her stomach. Had she just let a crazy person get into her car?

"Hannah," she said slowly, softly. "Are you alright tonight?"

"You have to listen to me!" Hannah shouted, now entirely losing any degree of cool she'd gained while trying to come down from her near panic attack.

Molly grew quiet.

"Why do you think Alex is in danger?" she asked. Molly couldn't deny that she'd had a funny feeling about the evening and still wanted Alex back in her care. But thoughts of the legend weren't at the top of her mind. More tucked into her subconscious wondering if Alex herself was scared, and if it had been the wisest decision to leave her with Melanie.

"I saw them," Hannah spoke, now seeming to try her best to sound reasonable. "They were all in the dining room. They were eating something. And Alex was there, gagged, tied up."

Molly gripped the steering wheel tighter. Now she hoped Hannah *was* crazy.

Still, she sped across town, headed for the McMasters House.

"It's all true," Hannah repeated. Though this time she sounded defeated.

Molly took it all in.

"Dr. Parsons was there," Hannah blurted out, as if remembering this for the first time. "He wrote something on Alex's chart and had me call a number I didn't know. Tell them we had what they were looking for."

This piqued Molly's curiosity. This felt real.

"Why Alex's chart?" she asked.

"Honestly, I don't know," Hannah said. "I think the phone call had something to do with what's happening tonight, though," she concluded.

Molly thought about the visit to Dr. Parsons office earlier that week. All they'd discussed was Alex's second spleen. That it ran in the family. Could that have something to do with what Hannah was trying to convince her of? This was batshit.

"I know it sounds crazy," Hannah said as they neared the edge of town, closing in on the McMasters residence. Molly could agree with that. But the detail about the phone call, and the fact that Hannah was very assertively telling her that Dr. Parsons was at the table where she saw Alex bound and gagged was alarming. It felt true and Molly wasn't sure why.

"Say that it is true," Molly said. "Should I just go to the door and ask for Alex?" she asked. "Or what do you propose we do?"

"I have a key to the house. I clean for them sometimes," Hannah said. "We can sneak in through a door that leads to the basement and embalming room."

Molly considered this.

This would be breaking and entering.

Was Alex really in danger? Was she being crazy? Was Hannah crazy?

But there was something deep in her gut that told her they

needed to get inside that house. Something was wrong. Perhaps it was just a mother's intuition. She thought she could feel it.

"What were they doing?" she asked Hannah, hoping for some piece of information that would sway her entirely. "Does this have to do with the genetic condition, Hannah?"

That was the part Molly couldn't quite dismiss.

"I think it does," Hannah said. "I think they wanted to take her spleen out."

"Why would they do that?" Molly asked, grasping for anything that might make her feel better about the whole thing.

"Well," Hannah tread carefully. "I think that's what was being eaten."

———

HANNAH TOLD Molly where to park. They exited the car, leaving it in a grassy patch on the side of the road about one-tenth of a mile from the funeral home. Hannah led the way but Molly kept close pace with her, both of them hurrying to get to the house.

"Where's the entrance?" Molly asked in a hushed tone.

Next to the funeral home was a cemetery, which Molly had always thought was humorously convenient. Now it didn't seem so humorous, just convenient.

The lights inside the house were on. Hannah grabbed Molly's hand and the pair of them crouched next to a head-stone at least one-hundred years old. Molly watched the house with Hannah.

Figures seemed to be moving to and fro in one of the upstairs rooms, their shapes silhouetted against ivory curtains that glowed yellow in the night.

"How do we get inside?" Molly repeated her question.

"See that little hill over there?" Hannah nodded toward a

tiny slope at the edge of the cemetery. "Just on the other side of that is a locked doorway that leads to an old tunnel that heads directly into the embalming room."

Molly thought about the strange visual Hannah had painted for her. The strange facts: Alex bound and gagged, something being eaten, and Hannah being sure that item was Alex's spleen.

But something deep down in Molly's gut told her that there was truth to this.

As soon as they unlocked that door, this would go from a crazy little adventure into breaking the law territory. And Molly felt okay about that.

Something wasn't right.

And then, something happened that sealed the deal for Molly.

They heard a scream from upstairs. A horrific animal sound that only meant agony or terror.

"Let's go," Molly told Hannah, and led the way to the door on the other side of the little hill.

———

THEY WERE in the tunnel within a minute, treading carefully, trying not to make too much noise. It was dank, dark, and everything Molly expected an ancient tunnel leading to an ancient embalming room would be. Hannah illuminated the passage with her cell phone's flashlight. It caught a spiderweb every few seconds. A couple of times Molly looked at the webs just fast enough to watch their makers crawl quickly out of sight behind a pipe that ran the length of the tunnel's ceiling.

Finally, they came to a door. The door to the embalming room. A caution symbol and a sign reading AUTHORIZED PERSONNEL ONLY greeted them.

Molly hadn't expected anything much warmer than that.

And it was probably about to get worse.

"Are you ready?" Hannah asked, ready to utilize her key once more.

Molly nodded, wordlessly. She sucked in a breath, preparing herself for whatever they might find on the other side of the door.

"I think we'll have an answer as to whether or not we should just get back into the car and leave once we open that door," Hannah said with trepidation.

Molly said a prayer, hoping that what they saw on the other side might make both of them feel incredibly foolish.

But when Hannah turned the key and the door creaked open, they found quite the opposite.

Bright fluorescent light flooded into the dank little tunnel, blinding Molly for a moment. She reached a hand to her forehead to block the light for a second. The contrast between the pitch black tunnel and the surgically lit embalming room sent an ache shooting out behind her eyeballs.

Finally she dropped her hand, her eyes adjusting to the brightness.

And what she saw sent her heart thundering in her chest.

The world almost went black. She swayed on her feet as they stepped inside.

Blood covered the floor. So much blood that Molly couldn't reconcile it with a dead person. This wasn't from an embalming.

"This looks like an emergency operating room," Hannah remarked.

"Is that normal?" Molly blurted out. "For a funeral home."

"No," Hannah said firmly. "This is not what a prep room should look like. Prep rooms are used for gently draining blood that flows down into a tube that goes to the sewer. Then pumping a body full of embalming fluid. You want the corpse to look as undisturbed as possible. This looks like someone had emergency surgery tonight."

"To have a spleen removed," Molly muttered. The feeling of dizziness left her in that moment. Wrath took over. The kind of ire that only a mother can feel when her child is in mortal danger. Something took the wheel. Every ounce of doubt and helplessness left Molly's body.

She turned to Hannah.

"Let's get my kid the fuck out of here," she said.

Hannah nodded.

"And I don't care if we have to kill someone to do it," she added.

Then the two of them headed for the door that led into the rest of the funeral home.

———

AS MOLLY GRABBED the handle of the door, she spoke softly to Hannah.

"Let's go upstairs," she said. "Towards the scream. If that was Alex, she's probably still up there."

There was no desperation in her voice. There was no doubt. There was nothing but determination. She would do what had to be done.

Hannah only nodded and pointed as they slowly cracked the door open. No one was in the hallway, but sound was coming from a room that seemed to be in another, far away, part of the house. That was reassuring. They should have time to go upstairs without anyone hearing the creaking of their footsteps.

Molly nodded and led the way, heading for the stairway at the end of the hallway in the direction Hannah had pointed. She took the stairs carefully, one at a time, but not entirely slowly. She moved with cat-like assurance and with purpose. Hannah kept up, closely on her heels.

They arrived on the first floor landing and Hannah pointed upwards.

They continued up, the sounds now on the same level they were on, the first floor. They echoed throughout the house. People talking. Not the sounds of a child's sleepover. Molly couldn't hear any children, for that matter.

She realized then that she hadn't seen the kids that were at the party. She wasn't even sure *if* there were any kids at the party.

It was another point that made her gut sink lower with the knowledge that something was very, very wrong and that her daughter was at the heart of it.

They reached the second story landing and the hallway was empty and quiet. This was the floor with the flurry of activity—with the scream—Molly thought. It was the floor where they'd seen the flutter of shadows just before that piercing sound.

Hannah pointed to one of the doors—all of them were closed—and Molly nodded, agreeing silently that she also thought that was their best place to start, judging from what they'd seen outside. That was probably the room.

The two of them stood in front of the door. Molly gave Hannah a look, almost like she was making sure the college-aged girl was still on board. They'd come this far.

Hannah nodded.

Molly opened the door slowly and it creaked loudly on its hinges. She grimaced, closed her eyes, as if she could silence it by sheer will. She pushed it further open and peeked into the room.

There was a woman lying on a bed, beneath covers, with a tiny lamp turned on by her bedside. Her chest rose and fell with shallow breaths. She was virtually unrecognizable, but Molly thought it was Melanie's mother.

The woman had children later in life, her mid-forties. The age could be right. She stood there silently staring at the woman for a moment. Suddenly, Hannah stumbled, stepping on Molly's shoe. The door swung wide open, making a horrendously loud creak.

The woman seemed to stir as the two of them found their footing, the door wide open now.

"Close it," Hannah whispered.

And Molly did.

The two of them stood there beside it, watching the woman. Her breathing grew more rapid, her eyes starting to search the room for some sign of whatever had made the noise. When she looked at Molly, in the dim lamplight, her eyes seemed to glow like two full harvest moons.

They were covered in milky cataracts.

The woman's eyes darted back and forth, searching the room for the sound she'd heard.

Molly and Hannah stood, frozen on the spot.

Molly thought that if the woman realized they were there —actually caught a glimpse of them—she might scream. Perhaps she was who they'd heard.

And then Molly realized that the woman was strapped to the iron bedframe beneath the twin mattress she was laying on. Her fear evaporated.

She rushed to her side.

"Hey," she said. "Hey, everything is okay."

The woman's eyes darted, searching for a clue as to who Molly was.

Then tears began to flow from her ghost-white eyes.

She sobbed and struggled against her bindings. Molly fiddled with the straps, trying to unbuckle the leather. Finally, she managed, and the old woman's hand went to her face, searching her features for familiarity.

And then, almost too low to hear, the sound obviously a huge effort for the woman, she spoke to Molly.

"It's me," she said.

Molly knelt beside the bed, puzzled. She looked back at Hannah, hoping that Hannah's medical field experience might provide them with some sort of guidance about how to handle the situation. Did the woman have dementia? Who did she think Molly was?

But when Hannah's eyes met hers, she saw that Hannah was terrified.

Her face had blanched, as ghostly pale as the woman's cataracts. Her eyebrows were high, her eyes wide open. Now she struggled to speak.

"What's wrong?" Molly asked the girl.

Hannah trembled, raising a hand to her throat as she spoke.

"That's the woman that I saw. Across the table from Alex," Hannah said quietly.

The woman dropped her hand from Molly's face and squeezed her arm tightly.

Molly turned to face the woman.

"You know the stories, Molly," Hannah said. "They're body snatchers."

Just then, the woman took Molly's hand in hers and traced something against her palm. A symbol that Molly would have recognized anywhere. A heart. The symbol Alex traced there when she was smaller. She would do it when she was stressed, tracing the symbol over and over until Molly was sure she was going to leave a blister.

"Oh, my God," Molly muttered.

The woman sobbed again, making incoherent attempts at speech.

"Oh, my *God*," Molly repeated.

The realization washed over her. It was almost so heavy that Molly was paralyzed, unsure of what to do next. But the old woman—was that Alex? Could that really be?—pointed to the corner of the room.

When Molly turned, she saw Alex's backpack, stuffed to the brim, sitting there.

She turned back to the body her daughter inhabited.

"Help," Alex croaked out of the dying woman's vocal cords.

Molly gripped her hand tightly, squeezing it with everything she had.

"I'm going to get you out of here," she whispered to her daughter.

Then she stood and faced Hannah.

"Okay," she said, sniffling away tears and swiping quickly at her eyes, not wanting Alex to perceive any of that. "We have some work to do."

Hannah only nodded.

———

"SO, IF SHE'S IN HERE," Molly murmured the words close to Hannah's face. "That means that whoever *she* was is inside my daughter?"

"I think that's what's happening, yes," Hannah confirmed. "I know it sounds crazy—"

"No," Molly said, rubbing her palm where moments before a heart had been traced there. "I believe you." She said this with certainty. Where earlier she'd been running on a mother's intuition, now she knew that her daughter needed her help in a very real way.

No matter how insane it might seem to anyone not within the walls of the McMasters Funeral Home.

Molly didn't have time to sort through the logical, rational gymnastics she would later do when this was over, trying to convince herself of what might have *really* been going on. Right now, she needed to figure out how to get her daughter back where she was supposed to be. Inside her own body.

"So what do we do now, Hannah?" Molly demanded.

She gave Hannah a hard stare, implying with just her eyes that Hannah better have an answer.

"I'm not a body snatching expert," Hannah blurted back, loudly.

"Shhhh!" Molly urged. She gestured at the body of the old woman in the bed in the corner.

Hannah quieted herself.

"Well," she said. "So they needed Alex's spleen, right?"

Molly nodded.

"And they ate it. This woman ate it," she pointed at the woman in the bed. "So, I think it has something to do with that. The consumption."

Molly thought about this.

"So, what if we reverse it?" she asked Hannah.

"What do you mean?" Hannah looked at her starkly, afraid of what Molly was implying, it seemed.

"What if I take the spleen out of the—person—Alex is inside?" she asked.

Hannah's face blanched once again.

"You mean—"

"Yes," Molly said firmly. "What if we feed it to the person inside of my daughter's body?" She looked at the woman— her daughter—laying in the bed in the corner, seeming to have drifted off to an exhausted sleep once more.

"I have no idea," Hannah said.

"She's dying," she pointed at the woman. "That old woman's body is dying. And if we don't do anything, my daughter is going to die inside of her."

Her tone grew firm but her voice held a tremor.

The possibility that Hannah might back out had occurred to her. She wasn't sure she could do this without any help whatsoever. She needed Hannah. At the very least to be a distraction.

She stared hard at Hannah. Hannah's eyes darted around the room, as if she'd find the answer scrawled on the wall. She looked back at Molly and sighed, resigned to her fate.

"I'll help you find her," she said to Molly.

Molly nodded.

That was good enough for now.

———

THEY LEFT the room where the woman—Alex—lay dying.

Molly knew that time was of the essence, and what she had implied that they would do began to sink in to her. One way or another, Molly's hands were going to have blood on them by the end of the night. And to reverse this, that meant she would have to open the old woman's body and feed her spleen to Alex. Or to the person inhabiting Alex's body.

And it was highly unlikely that whoever was inhabiting her daughter's body at the moment was going to eat willfully.

The whole thing would be messy.

It seemed ludicrous. Insane. Like it surely had to be some divorce-induced waking nightmare.

Maybe Molly would wake up in a moment, sweaty in her own bed, Alex in the other room.

But she doubted it.

They went back downstairs, following the sounds of voices.

"We need a weapon," Hannah whispered to Molly, grabbing her wrist as Molly tried to head for the sounds of the voices. "And something to knock the old woman out with."

Molly looked back at her and considered this. She was right.

"The embalming room," Hannah suggested.

Once there, Hannah opened the door with her key again. The same key that had let them in from the outside. The door locked on its own every time it shut, keeping people from wandering into something they might not want to see, Hannah explained.

Once inside, they began to look around.

Molly found a drawer with scalpels. She grabbed one.

There were other tools of the trade that looked as though they hadn't been updated since the time of the Ancient Egyptians. One of which was a pair of forceps that were disturbingly long and curved slightly at the end.

"Ah-ha!" Hannah said.

Molly whipped around to see Hannah fiddling with something attached to one of the embalming tanks. At the end of the hose, Hannah wrestled off a long, needle-looking object. She held it up proudly.

It was sharp at one end and hollow just like a needle.

"They use it to suck the blood out from the organs," Hannah said. "It's strong enough to stab someone."

Molly nodded.

"Perfect," she said.

Molly found a pair of sharp scissors. With those, her scalpel, and the forceps, she felt she was as prepared as she was going to get.

"Let's go," she told Hannah.

Hannah grabbed something else. A small container and a rag.

"Chloroform," she said darkly.

Molly only nodded.

And the pair of them went to face their fate.

———

THE VOICES WAFTED down the hall, Melanie's laugh punctuating some joke.

Molly felt rage rise in her chest. The desire to just claw the woman's eyes out, ask no questions and take no prisoners.

But it wasn't that simple. She needed to be sure of what she was doing. She needed her daughter's soul back inside her rightful body. Which she knew was likely standing in the room with Melanie.

Finally, they reached the doorway. Molly caught sight of

Melanie for a half-second. She jerked back, putting an arm out to keep Hannah against the wall next to her.

She looked at Hannah, holding up a hand to tell her to wait for just a little bit longer.

And then she nodded.

She stepped around the doorway, the scissors in her hand, held by the handle, the blades pointing downward like a weapon.

"Hello," she said, interrupting the conversation taking place.

Melanie turned, clearly unnerved by the sudden departure from whatever conversation they were having.

Molly kept her eyes on Melanie for a moment, sizing her up and making sure she was unarmed, which she seemed to be.

"Where's my daughter?" she demanded of the woman.

Hannah crept up beside her.

"What do you mean?" Melanie asked, her voice faltering only the tiniest amount.

Molly looked around the room and didn't see Alex. Her stomach dropped slightly.

What if she was already gone?

"Where is she?!" Molly shouted and the room fell silent. She held up the scissors.

She spotted Dr. Parsons sitting across the room. A woman was with him. She looked like a chemotherapy patient and she clung to Parsons.

His wife, likely.

"What the hell are you doing here?" Molly asked.

"Molly, why don't you sit down?" Melanie said, stepping forward.

Molly held out the scissors.

"Don't fucking touch me, bitch," she muttered as Melanie dropped the hand that had been reaching for Molly's arm.

Something shifted in Melanie's eyes.

"They're just having a slumber party," she said, false lightness in her voice.

Just then, the pattering of feet came running down the hallway. Two girl's voices intermingling, one of which Molly recognized instantly.

They barreled around the corner, boxing Hannah and Molly into the stateroom where everyone was gathered. Sylvia first, then Alex—or whomever was inhabiting her body. The pair of them looked at Molly.

"Alex," she said to her daughter.

The girl looked at her with eyes that didn't register her. She was seeing Molly, but she didn't know her. The girl glanced at Melanie, as if for a cue.

"Alex," Molly said more firmly. "Is that you?" she asked.

"Molly, are you feeling well?" Melanie asked, again attempting to intervene.

"I'm fine," she said without looking away from her daughter's body.

The girl—Alex—looked once again at Melanie, as if asking for help. She jerked away from Molly as she reached for her.

"You're not my daughter," Molly said to the girl.

Something registered on the girl's face then. On Alex's familiar features. But it wasn't Alex. The expression was entirely someone else's, manipulating the muscles on her daughter's face in ways that weren't Alex's. It was whoever was inside of her.

And Molly intended to get that person out.

And get her daughter back into her body.

She reached for the girl's wrist, but she backed away too quickly.

Melanie seized the opportunity, shoving Molly down and grabbing the scissors when they skittered over the carpet. She pinned her down.

"Stop!" Hannah shouted, hovering above them, the

embalming tool firmly in her hands, raised over her head. "Let her go or I'll fucking stab you," she said to Melanie.

Melanie looked up and barked out a laugh at first.

"Sorry," she said. "It's just that I never saw you as any kind of heroine, Hannah. More of a victim of your circumstances."

She began to speak to Hannah in a way that Molly knew was manipulation. She watched as Hannah's grip on the giant needle faltered.

"Staying in your home town when everyone else went out to see the world. Dating one loser after another. Dropping out of college not once but twice. You're going to end up as fat and unhappy as your mama," Melanie said so viciously that bile coated each word and they hung heavily in the air.

"Melanie, that's unnecessary," Dr. Parsons stood, shaking off his wife's grip.

"You shut the hell up," Melanie said. "The whole reason you're here is for this," she gestured at Alex. "You want the same for your dying wife just like I wanted it for my dying mother."

The facade had crumbled, leaving only raw, jagged truth behind in its rubble.

Molly struggled against Melanie, worming her way out from under her. But Melanie returned her focus to the woman beneath her. She leaned down harder with her pelvis, straddling Molly's upper abdomen, now holding the scissors.

Molly remembered something then.

"You don't need to do this, Melanie," Dr. Parsons was now in full on hostage negotiation mode.

Melanie shifted her focus back to Dr. Parsons long enough for Molly to slowly reach for her pocket. Where she had tucked the scalpel and the forceps. She withdrew the first and waited a moment longer as Melanie and Dr. Parsons bickered, his wife begging him not to get involved in the background.

And as Melanie turned back, Molly slashed at her face. First one direction, then the other.

Melanie screamed, throwing herself off of Molly. Molly scrambled to her feet and reached once again for the woman commandeering her daughter's body. She grabbed her by the wrist.

Melanie screamed again and Dr. Parsons grabbed her, half-restraining her and half-tending to her wounds. Molly didn't bother to look to see the damage.

The little girl—the person inside of Alex—bit her hard on the hand. The one with which she gripped the girl's wrist.

Molly cried out at the sensation of the girl's teeth breaking her skin. And then the girl ran out of the room. Sylvia followed her.

"Wait, grandma!" she called.

It was confirmation of everything that Molly already knew to be true.

She stood upright, grasping her bleeding hand and turned to Hannah.

"Stay here," she told Hannah. "Don't let her out of your sight," she instructed. "I'll get her."

Hannah nodded, a dark expression traded between the two of them,

Hannah handed her the chloroform and rag, and then Molly set out into the hall to track the girls down.

Alex was strong, her body and her mind. Fighting her to the ground would be a feat.

Forcing her to eat something she didn't want to eat would be another thing entirely.

And then subduing Sylvia. Things had gotten complicated quickly.

She tracked the sound of footsteps up the stairs. Finally, she heard the girls' voices.

"Shhh!" the woman inside of Alex's body urged her granddaughter.

It was too late, though. Molly knew where they were.

But she wasn't sure she was ready to face the reality in front of her. She couldn't think about it too much.

She rounded the corner, entering the room upstairs. A bedroom. A little girl's bedroom. Sylvia's. She stepped inside, straining her ears for any sign of movement.

A stifled sob came from beneath the bed. Likely the younger of the two girls—the only one of them that was actually a little girl. She heard the sound of the other one—the old woman inside her daughter's body—clapping a hand over the little girl's mouth, silencing her.

Molly walked around to the other side of the bed and spotted a shoe sticking out.

She reached down in a sharp motion and yanked the leg the shoe belonged to.

The girl yelled—her daughter's voice, but not her daughter—and Molly did everything she could to not think about it. To not try to understand what she was seeing—physically, her daughter; in reality, a monster—and she pulled her out from under the bed.

She straddled her. Sylvia screamed as her companion was captured. She scrambled out from under the bed and took off down the hallway.

Molly returned her focus to her daughter—or the person inhabiting her body.

She needed to get her back to the room where Alex was. Her soul, at least.

With no time to get the chloroform, she grabbed the lamp on the nightstand and yanked it out of the wall. Six seconds, that's all it takes. She remembered Mark saying that after they came home from a Brazilian jiu-jitsu class that they took together in those last attempts that Molly made to save their marriage.

He'd been fascinated with that—the short amount of time

it took to put someone to sleep—meanwhile Molly had wondered if it would ever be useful.

And here she was, wrapping the electrical cord of the lamp around the neck of her daughter's struggling body.

She wrapped it once, then twice, and then twisted it, creating a secure garotte. And she held it. Counting down.

Six.

Five.

Four.

Three.

Two.

One.

———

ALEX'S BODY went limp after six seconds. Molly quickly undid the garotte, allowing for the oxygen in her blood to return to her brain. She had to move quickly. The scalpel was still in her pocket, tucked there on her way out of the state room, headed for the room where Melanie and the others were.

She hurried, making quick work of the distance. She threw the door open to the room where Alex's soul was, trapped in that old woman's horrible body. And if Molly didn't act quickly, her daughter would die.

The old woman—Alex—groaned in her sleep, waking slowly at the sound of activity near her.

Molly glanced at the woman's body that housed her daughter's soul.

She looked back at the girl in her arms—Alex's body with someone else's consciousness at the helm. The whole situation was surreal. Almost entirely beyond computation.

She knew what she had to do.

She laid Alex's body down on the floor. She got chloroform onto the rag. She grasped the scalpel in her hand. She said a quick prayer that Hannah was doing well holding everyone downstairs.

She fought against the thought that this was lunacy.

This was criminal.

This could be murder.

She knew with all that she was—deep in her gut—that this was right.

This was what she had to do.

She walked over to the bed. She couldn't bear to wake Alex. This has to happen quickly. She smothered her with the rag, watching as she slowly drifted into a deeper sleep. It made Molly sick.

She pulled the old woman's night-shirt up. She pressed her fingers against her abdomen.

And then Molly brought the scalpel down.

She cut in the right place. A place that she was all too familiar with from years of her own tests and years of her daughter's. She knew exactly where the spleen was. She remembered countless nights that she laid awake, poking at her own abdomen, trying to feel the second organ inside of herself.

And then plunged the scalpel in, forsaking any reason that might have prevented her from doing it.

"It's okay," Molly whispered to the unmoving body before her.

Time was of the essence. She had to be alive when she force-fed the organ to the girl.

She worked quickly as she began the nasty business of extracting the spleen, all while listening to the sounds of the girl on the floor coming back to life.

———

MOLLY'S EYES unfocused as she performed her task. The edges of neatly sliced skin and fat were blurry. It felt like a dream. Or a nightmare, rather. Her hands were slick with blood by the time the spleen was being held by both of them. The organ was smaller than she'd anticipated, yet still somehow the most important thing she'd ever held.

She walked to the spot on the floor where the woman in her daughter's body laid, blood dripping onto the ivory carpet. The old woman in the bed moaned—no, *Alex* moaned— with barely enough life left in her to survive the next half hour, which would be necessary. She was beginning to wake.

She reached with one blood-slick hand and shook the girl with vigor. She woke, slowly. Her eyes searching the room for any source of light that might let her know what was happening.

"Eat," Molly said, her voice shaking.

There was commotion downstairs. Something crashed, glass shattered. There was shouting and Molly thought it was in Hannah's voice.

Time was of the essence.

Molly knelt next to her daughter's body. She grabbed for her jaw. The woman inside fought her like a tiger, clawing, biting at Molly. She roared in terror and anger. She knew what it would mean for her to eat the diseased spleen that once belonged to her.

It would mean death.

And life for Alex.

Molly ripped at the spleen, tearing off a piece and shoving it into the girl's mouth. She spat it out. Thundering footsteps bounded up the stairs. Molly worked quickly, hoping that she could race against time.

She clapped a hand over the girl's mouth when she shoved the piece back in, fuzzy with strands of carpet. She forced her to swallow by holding her nose. The girl fought and writhed, clawed at Molly's hands. But Molly held on, blood dripping from her arms now—her own.

Molly worked piece by piece, quickly, forcing them down the girl's throat.

The door was flung wide open. Molly looked up to see Dr. Parsons, Melanie right on his heels.

"Stop!" Melanie demanded, trying to step past Dr. Parsons.

"Do not come in here," Molly said, biting off each word as its own statement.

Dr. Parsons reached to stop Melanie just as Molly forced the last piece of the spleen down the girl's throat. Molly jumped back, putting space between herself and Melanie.

Melanie darted to the girl. To Alex's body.

Molly looked at the old woman's body in the bed across the room.

She was still. Molly rushed to the woman's side, taking her hand.

"Alex," she said. "Alex?" It was a demand. A demand that her daughter hold on, just a little bit longer. The woman seeped blood from the incision, so much that Molly wasn't sure there would be enough left for her to remain alive long enough for the switch to take place. She held her breath.

"You whore," the girl said from across the room.

It was Alex's voice but not Alex.

Molly looked over at her. The girl stared at her, daggers in her eyes. The knowledge of what was going to happen washed over her.

She shook Melanie off and lunged for Molly. She swiped the scalpel from the nightstand where Molly had left it. She slashed, chasing Molly to the far corner of the room.

"Enough!" Dr. Parsons shouted.

"No!" the girl screeched. But now, her voice—Alex's voice—was breaking. Something was happening. The old woman in the bed sputtered, coughing up blood. Then she howled. She made noises like a dying animal. It was happening.

The girl's face changed then. It fell. The mask of muscle

movements that did not belong to Molly's daughter faded and were replaced by something familiar.

Alex.

"Oh, my God," Molly breathed. Tears flooded her eyes.

The girl—now her daughter once more—dropped the scalpel to the floor. Molly reached down, grabbed it, then hugged Alex.

Alex squeezed her so tightly that it made the tears flow more freely.

"What's going on?" Hannah called from the doorway.

Molly and Alex spun, looking at her. Dr. Parsons did the same as Melanie rushed to her dying mother's bedside.

"No!" Melanie cried out now.

"Let's get the fuck out of here," Hannah said to Molly.

"Save her!" Melanie shouted to Dr. Parsons.

He went to the woman's side. She'd grown still.

"She's gone, Melanie," he told her.

"Let's go!" Hannah shouted once again.

"Wait," Molly said. She pushed Alex towards Hannah. She walked over to Melanie, the scalpel still in her hand. She pointed it at her and Dr. Parsons.

The two of them looked at her, Dr. Parsons with fear in his eyes. Melanie was furious.

"Listen to me, and listen carefully," Molly said. "She died tonight," she pointed at the old woman in the bed. "Tragic. Her body just gave out. Dr. Parsons happened to be here and tried to intervene, but it didn't work." Molly went on. "And we were not here." She gestured at her daughter, Hannah, and herself.

Dr. Parsons nodded immediately, likely thinking of his medical license.

"You will move away from here," Molly said to him, fiercely. "You will start over somewhere else. Maybe you'll retire and take care of your dying wife like you should."

He looked at her sheepishly, entirely under her persuasion and nodded.

"And you," she pointed the scalpel now at Melanie, who stood up, defiant. "I don't care where you go. I don't care what you do. But you don't live in this town anymore. You or Sylvia. You'll sell the funeral home and you'll go. But you will not stay here."

Melanie looked like she was about to give Molly a piece of her mind. The two slashes from the scalpel still bled freely down her face. Dr. Parsons reached for her.

"Listen to her, Melanie," he said. "She's serious."

Molly cracked a smile. She wondered if it had ever occurred to Mark what she was capable of.

Highly unlikely.

"We're going to leave now," she said, glancing at her daughter and Hannah. "And if I ever see either of you again, I'll fucking kill you. How's that for a fair deal?"

Dr. Parsons nodded once more. Melanie glared at her, but finally acquiesced.

"It's over," Molly said to Melanie. "No more."

Melanie breathed sharply in through her nose, seeming to know the score. That she was defeated. And she resigned herself to her fate. She cried, swiping at her eyes. Then she turned to leave the room, presumably to find her daughter.

Dr. Parsons left and Molly, Hannah, and Alex headed for the front door.

———

THE OLD MCMASTERS woman was buried in the next few days.

It was in those days afterwards that Molly pieced everything together. The double organ. That she was meant to supply her own spleen for Dr. Parsons' wife. Alex told her what she'd heard—that they needed people with double organs to keep the host viable after the consumption took place. They'd used the old woman as proof for Dr. Parsons and his wife. She wondered if money was going to change hands. A price on her daughter's life. A price on her own.

Dr. Parsons stole away in the night, abandoning his practice abruptly.

She didn't see Melanie but once.

She spotted her loading things into one of the hearses. There was also a U-Haul parked outside the funeral home. It went up for sale within days. Molly sat, hidden in some trees, watching as Melanie loaded up the last of their belongings and hit the road with Sylvia.

Molly planned to keep tabs on both Melanie and Dr. Parsons.

But as she sipped her coffee, her phone rang. The divorce attorney.

"Hello?" Molly said, instinctively.

"Mrs. Southard," the woman said. "I have bad news."

Molly felt nothing. Not a stab of trepidation. Nothing.

"Your husband isn't agreeing to the settlement. Do you want to fight him on this?"

Molly felt a small smile curve her lips. Something had happened in the last few days. A rekindling of who she used to be. A rebirth. She spoke confidently.

"We'll fight him on it," she said. "And we'll win."

The Legend of Jeanie Knight

Collette Carmon

Boy

I suppose the "legend" starts the way all others do. Around a bonfire, with drunken idiots who don't know shit about life. This one has been around since before my parents, rising in the generation of my great-grandparents. During that "Gilded Age of America". The time when women weren't considered creatures worth autonomy—when they hoarded jewelry because they couldn't have bank accounts, they were unable to purchase things without a man and were generally regarded as prized ponies for trade or sale. And I've often wondered if the legend was born from the frustration of a girl—or group of girls—in this town.

Even now, as I listen to Braden regale a group of Freshies with The Legend of Jeanie Knight, I feel sorry for the women who needed a fictional savior. One who came to slay their mental dragons, even if Jeanie couldn't slay the monsters of their reality.

Jeanie was a name synonymous with vengeance in this town, and as such there had not been a Jeanie who was born here or christened here since the story rose from dust. Jeanie became a holy moniker none dared to bestow upon their daughters, for fear of the doom she would bring those around her.

Foolish bullshit, but no one ever asked for my opinion. So I kept that opinion to myself as Braden made the two girls squeal with his tale. The booze in their Solo cups sloshing when they bounce and release delighted screams, listening intently as he tells them of how Jeanie Knight drains her victims. A vampire in some versions, a woman in white in others, a witch in the halls of the local church…where girls chant Jeanie's name instead of Mary's when the lights go out in the bathrooms.

> *She came at night,*
> *To haunt the town,*
> *Wearing a bloody gown*
> *And crown,*
> *Delighted laughter*
> *Beneath the moon,*
> *Jeanie Knight will be your doom.*

"ON GOD," Braden swears with a vicious sort of grin. One that seems sharper and more pronounced as the fire lights across the edges of his face. A demon in his own right, but I also hold tight to that opinion as I accept an unopened beer from Adam. Another of my varsity teammates. He rolls blue eyes at Braden's flirtatious ways and chuckles when he sees that I've noticed.

"Dude is nearly nineteen, what's he thinkin' hittin' on Freshies?" Adam asks me, a few beers later when Braden doesn't let up and has drawn both girls down onto his lap.

"I don't ask, man. Not my business," I tell Adam with a

pointed glance in Braden's direction. "The less you worry about what he's doing the better off you are."

Adam frowns, "Even if it's wrong?"

"Good men don't win, bro, that's the movies talking. In real life, the Braden's of the world are coming out on top. So you're either in their good graces or you're on the outs." One of the few lessons my father taught before his departure from my life.

Adam's expression remains sour, but eventually, he concedes. His blue eyes dart away from the line of trees Braden disappears behind with one of the girls, and there's a heaviness that blankets the area around us. The tension remains even after I pass him a bottle of Jack. Whiskey doesn't help take off the edge, but it can make someone forget for a bit.

TIME IS irrelevant in the woods. The fire blazes, the night deepens, and stars come out into the clearing. Some of my teammates continue swapping locker room stories. Ones that I don't join because it makes me uncomfortable to kiss and tell, but I'd be lying if I said I didn't enjoy hearing about some of their escapades. I'd be lying if I said I didn't enjoy the pictures that get passed around on cell phones. A few times, I'm greeted with the images of girls I myself have known, and an uncomfortable feeling grips my chest. It feels like inadequacy and self-repugnance. Did he know her before me? After? During?

Does it matter?

Some part of me believes it does, but my mother would rage against me if she knew I thought such things. She's got a thing about people born with vaginas being the better of the two physical genders, and when she starts on gender norms and other shit, I tune her out. Dad left me with her and she hates me for the one appendage I didn't ask for.

Maybe I hate women, a small bit, as a result.

Maybe that's why, when an hour passes, after Braden's and Freshie's departure into the trees, I don't go looking for them. Maybe, in some quiet, horrible part of myself, I am happy that she's being hurt.

Because I know Braden.

He's one of the nameless monsters in The Legend of Jeanie Knight. A boy with a gilded future—an athlete, a spoiled son of a man with money and power, a boy who was never taught to respect women.

A *rapist.*

The word never passes any of our lips, but we know what Braden is. We knew the first time he assaulted one of the freshmen who tried out for the team in our junior year. We knew it when his girlfriend broke up with him and left town. We knew it when his sister's best friend and her brother quit coming around. Braden likes power. He enjoys knowing that they will never tell…

Even if they do, he knows nothing will come of his games. Braden is a prince in this town. Who would dare stop him?

That's what I think when I hear that girl's scream as it echoes through the night.

"Help me," she cries. The sound of something shattering as we all pretend not to hear her—laughing and passing bottles around the fire. "Please help me," she screams again, followed by Braden's mocking laughter.

"No one is coming for you, sweet tha-ng," he taunts with a loud voice. We all hear him, but not a single one of us moves to help her. Not even Adam who looks as if he is on the verge of crying…destroyed by what he hears.

"Please," we can hear her when we all fall silent. Each trapped in our own hell of mourning—cowards is what we are.

"Please, save me, Jeanie…" and Braden's laughter following that awful plea is the worst sound of all.

If Jeanie is real, we deserve to die by her hand.

———

SCHOOL STARTS the same way it always does. Too early and too loud. It is as if nothing has changed, but I am aware of the shift in the halls. The tension that surrounds us as a collective. A tension born from a secret we all share. One that no one speaks, but everyone knows.

Braden is the only one unbothered by this horror show he's created. A caricature of happiness and perfect living. He moves through the halls with his usual devil-may-care attitude. Laughing at jokes he hears as he leads a pack of football players. I'm not among them today, I'm still hungover. The only way I can stomach facing my mother is fucked up, and she is so oblivious that she never notices. So I watch my peers, boys I have considered friends for years, laugh and yell about shit I don't care think on at this moment. I care about taking a nap or eating a handful of Tylenol to chase away this headache.

"You okay?" Someone asks me, a smoky voice I don't recognize.

Even still I reply, "Yeah, just tired."

I turn, finding a dark-haired girl with wide honey-colored eyes. I don't recognize her, which isn't totally unusual—the school is large and there are people who don't register on my radar. What is unusual is that I have never noticed a girl like her before. She's all feline grace and her beauty is more than aesthetically pleasing. It's like she's cut from a different cloth of time and a better ream of fabric.

"Can I help you get somewhere? You look green," she continues, unaware of my appraisal of her person.

I grunt, allowing her to help me with my bag as I tell her I just need to see the nurse. Despite being ill, I'm the one who leads the way.

"Are you new?" I ask though I've got a feeling that she has to be. Everyone knows where the nurse's office is—people skip class there all the time because our school nurse is a lax, uncaring woman who is lucky to still have a medical license.

"I am, but that doesn't mean I will ignore a stranger in duress." Her smile is soothing. Almost maternal—if I knew what a maternal smile was meant to look like.

"Thanks," I tell her as we enter the door that leads to the nurse's office. She hands me my bag, her fingers brushing mine and I must have a fever because her touch is cold. Like ice courses through her veins.

"No problem," she smiles and I am lured to sea with that smile. Something in her calls to something in me, and I feel like a fool as I stand there gaping. She chuckles, "I need to get to class…but I'll see you around," she trails off clearly expecting me to fill in my name.

"Todd," I supply, my name heavy and clumsy on my tongue. As if it's the first time I've ever spoken my own name, and the way I trip over myself causes her to smile again.

"What about you?" I ask as she starts up the emptying halls. The second bell ringing some moments before.

She turns back to me, those honey eyes holding me captive as she says, "Jean."

I watch her go, a sense of foreboding coming over me due to her name. A shorter, similar name to the one that rang out in the night three times. As Braden assaulted the girl whose name I have yet to learn.

Jeanie, help me.

Jeanie, save me.

Jeanie, kill them all…

Pleas that Braden mocked, amused by her fear, and the reminder churns my gut. I want to forget that sound.

I've known about Braden for nearly as long as I've known him. We've remained friendly enough for me to stay on his good side, but distant enough that the guy doesn't decide to assault me in his dad's pool house with a pool cue. Yet, according to him, we are *best friends*. A terrifying notion, but I roll with it because I've always heard it's better to keep one's enemies closer than one's friends. Braden is a frenemy I'd like to keep tabs on at all times.

As if summoned by the mere thought of him, a text comes through my phone. His name on my screen fills me with discomfort, but I open the message as I flop onto the hard, thin cot the nurse keeps for sleeping off her own hangovers. I don't blame her, her husband is fucking around on her with the newer edition of herself. I'd drink myself into oblivion too if that were my life.

Braden's text is a series of images I didn't want to see. Yet, they will be burned into my mind along with those horrible screams.

She's got the body of a girl that has morphed between child and woman, and I'm torn between disgust and intrigue —something that deepens my self-hatred.

I've seen nakedness before, but there's something worse about it when you know the person being photographed is a victim of a crime. Her face is agony. Terror and hatred. Things that probably excite a devil like Braden.

Todd, I think I was her first, how sweet is that? The text reads. I read it over three times.

Wondering what it must feel like to have a first time rooted in violence. My first was awkward for both of us. Bumbling virgins who laughed and apologized a lot during knocking limbs and strange sensations. That was normal, even if embarrassing to look back on. This is something else. This is something from which she will never recover. Even if this girl is healed, physically, and works to heal herself mentally. Braden will always be there. He will be in her, a weed that cannot be killed or unrooted.

I've passed it around to all the guys. Braden brags when I don't respond. *So you pussies can be jealous.*

I'm bent over the trashcan when the nurse comes in, losing the little food in my belly as bile burns my throat when that's all I have left to give.

———

ADAM HAS that frown on his face, the one that tells me he's not in a good mood when I walk into the locker rooms after practice. A shitshow due to my dehydration and hangover. Coach wasn't thrilled, but there were worse performers on the field—sparing me from the brunt of his ire. Adam's I won't miss, clearly, when he stands up from one of the benches and marches towards me.

He shoves me into the metal, slamming my shoulder into one of the metal door latches. I hiss, but before I can curse him and his mother, Adam growls.

"You need to stop him."

Ah, I realize, *this anger is not mine.*

"You stop him," I hiss back. When fear flits across Adam's face I release a condescending laugh, "That's what I thought. You're scared to try, so don't come in here acting like I've gotta do what you don't got the balls to do."

He releases me, sagging back down onto the bench, "Did you see what he sent us?"

The images burn across my memory, assaulting my mind as those screams flood through me. As if they are happening again.

"Yeah," I reply. Knowing that if I keep talking about it or if I keep remembering I will lose what little lunch I was able to choke down.

"We need to tell someone," Adam whispers. As if he's confessing to a priest—a great sin from which he needs absolution. I wish my heart was that clear, that kind.

It's not.

I'm doing good to put anyone I love above myself, let

alone some girl I don't know. I feel sorry for her, but not enough to mess with my future. Braden's dad is a powerful criminal defense attorney. He'd have me working for scraps in a dive kitchen, in a moment, if he thought I was going to betray his son.

No.

One girl is not worth my future. She isn't worth jeopardizing my way out of this shit hole.

"You can tell; if you want to be stupid. I'm not. She's not worth making waves and, to be honest, Braden won't get in trouble even if you tell. He's going to fuck with you if he thinks you ratted him out." Adam looks up at me, fear draining the sun-kissed color from his face.

"You won't tell him we talked about this, will you?"

"No, man, I'm not a fucking rat." I leave him in the sweat-soaked locker room. The scent of adolescence and cheap Irish Spring soap—of all the memories that should flood into me from those scents, I know that this moment with Adam will be the one that flows the strongest. Self-disgust is a strong memory motivator…my mother's greatest lessons were meted through shame. Those are the ones that have resonated with me the longest.

———

BRADEN STOPS by my house after my mom leaves for her overnight shift. She works at one of those loony bins where they always have to have a psychologist on site. It means there are long periods of time where I don't see her, and I'm perfectly fine with her absences. They were rough after Dad left, but now they're old hat. I wouldn't want her near me until I've had time to process and school my face against revealing Braden's newest evil. I don't need her deciding to damn me as an accomplice and sniff out a weakness.

"Adam's a fucking downer, man," he complains as he flops

down onto the expensive sofa in my mom's sitting area. The one she expressly forbids me from using when I have people over.

I don't dare tell Braden to get off of the suede. He'd just laugh and do something ultra incriminating like urinate on the cushions out of spite.

"Why," I ask, feigning innocence.

"He asked me not to send him pics and vids again. As if he didn't fucking like them or something," Braden snorts and pulls a flask from the inside pocket of his letterman jacket. The whiskey has a sharp, smoky scent I can detect between us even though I'm standing across the room. One of his father's favorite barrels that are always aged to perfection. Braden steals without consequence, unafraid of his father's ire. He takes a deep draw and smacks his lips as if he hasn't just gulped down expensive liquor with the same regard for it that he has for cheap McCormick's rum.

"Man, maybe just let the kid alone, you know how he is," I tell him, turning away so that Braden doesn't notice my discomfort.

"Yeah, fuckin' virgin," Braden snorts, and my stomach turns with the flippant way that he says those words. As if he didn't steal something girls are told they are supposed to protect. Misguided purity that will add to her shame, my mom is in my head. Whispering I'm a failure of a human for not being decent enough to put a fellow man in his place.

"Yeah," I agree because I'm a coward.

I open the door to the liquor cabinet, grabbing the whiskey, the light catches the liquid, lightening it to the color of burnt honey. The shade reminds me of Jean's eyes.

Jeanie, I think as I drink down a swig.

Jeanie, I think as I watch Braden cackling on my mother's expensive sofa.

Jeanie, I think as I follow Braden to the door…watching him climb into his brand new Mustang and leave.

A DRUNKEN HAZE leads me on a journey I don't remember, but I wake from that fog in a familiar cemetery. The one that lies off the old, forked road that runs along the edge of this nowhere town. Rotted leaves and the crispness of the world, as it begins to die for the winter's long mourning. Scents that assault my senses while fear trickles down my spine with the slithering path of cold sweat. Headstones turn sinister beneath the bright moon, throwing angles of weathered marble into sharp relief. I've never been frightened of land filled with the dead. My father used to bring me on "night hunts" searching amongst the tombstones for little trinkets he'd left around to fill me with childish delight.

Now there's something strange here, a magic that leaves me unsettled—heavy—and I notice where I stand. The iron bands cross over the grave. An ancient precaution against something *other. Something not human.* A witch, a woman in white...

A vampire.

I turn, and as the word moves through my mind. I see *her.*

Jean.

Her dark hair melts into the night where the moonlight doesn't glitter off of the strands, her eyes beneath that same light become molten gold as she stares into my soul, but it's her mouth that paralyzes me.

A grinning mouth, full of razor teeth, that drips with thick, rust-red blood.

She glances down, to a body at her feet, and my eyes follow her line of sight. A scream lodges itself in my throat, choking and silent, as I take in the white leather letterman sleeves, stained with blood. A curly top of hair I know so well, and the blood-marred number 24 patch, tells me this body is Adam's.

I'm still, watching in a paralyzed state, as Jean marches

towards me. Her steps a funeral march that is a haunting melody of crunching leaves beneath the hard soles of her shoes. She's so close, when she stops, that I can smell the blood on her putrid breath. "Do you want to know how he tastes?" She asks me, with a voice so soft, so serene. A sound that should not come from the tongue of a monster.

I don't answer, my throat closes around each word I'd want to speak.

My silence doesn't faze Jean, her grin opens wider, spreading impossibly large—seeming to split her face into two as her teeth are exposed to the moonlight.

"He tastes like weakness," her expression hardens. Her words turn serious as her voice loses that gentle, serene edge. The monster comes out of her now. An unmasked entity as she falls into all of her rage.

I want to ask her *why* but neither my mouth nor my tongue will cooperate.

"He deserved to die, same as the rest of them do for listening to that girl and remaining silent." She answers, as if she's read my mind, and presses closer. The sticky blood on her hands stains my throat as she pulls me closer, fingers dancing up into the hair at the base of my neck while she yanks me to her. Against my slack mouth, she places a kiss that tastes like death. Pushing what she took from Adam into me with gentle violence.

As she pulls back, her grin wide and sharklike, and I shudder. Adam's blood congealing on my skin while Jean laughs. The moonlight glints off of her body, shining on her blood-stained lips, and I wonder if she is a devil come to life.

Her gaze slips over me, an oily caress I'd like to burn off of my skin.

———

HOW I MAKE my way home, I'll never know. Jean leaving me alive fills me with dread.

The bathroom mirror tells a story of violence. One I didn't commit, but there I stand, covered in the remnants of a crime. Blood clings to every part of me, my clothes, my skin… beneath my nails after I try to scratch it off of myself.

Anxiety fills me, pounding in my throat, as I think of what my mother will think should she arrive home. Seeing me covered with blood and panicked. No doubt she would paint me the villain in this story. A monster who deserves the hammer of justice. Despite the fact, I am the witness, not the perpetrator of destruction.

I have to clean this up…before Mother finds out.

I strip naked and take my compromised clothing to the living room. It's chilly enough this time of year that a fire isn't unheard of, and I use that to my advantage. Starting the logs from the last one, adding my clothes on top of them, and stacking fresh logs over them.

Burn, hurry up and burn.

I want them destroyed, as fast as possible. My heartbeat pounds in my ear, louder than a bass drum, kicking out a speedy rhythm I'm not sure anyone could recreate. The fire slowly eats away at the cotton of my clothing, an unpleasant stench that assaults my senses.

A scent that hits me with a memory, one that swims and moves the room around me. I stagger, willing it away as it hits harder, the stench of blood fills me, so much of it I might as well be drowning in an ocean of thick, slippery liquid that tastes of death and life.

Hold still, little bitch!

The voice is loud, full of anger and hatred as it covers me. Filling me as the feeling of the rough, painful grip of hands hold me too tight. My back remembers the hardness of the ground, the bite of grit against my bare skin. Nails cutting into my thighs.

"No," I scream, an incantation that flows out of me with the force of an avenging angel. Effectively stopping whatever evil memory is trying to invade me.

Stay here, safe here, stay here.

A mantra fills my mind, a voice I both do and do not recognize. Young, feminine, unsettling. A voice that stills, suddenly quiet, when the doorbell rings.

Ignoring the summoning, I glance at the pile of my clothing, nearly all of it a char of fresh ash. Soothed by the image, evidence destroyed, I turn, fleeing towards the stairwell. Each step brings me closer to the bathroom, where I turn the shower on too hot. Allowing the heat to scorch off my skin, turning the water that swirls the drain a pink tint as the stream reddens my skin.

Wash away the sins, it's that same voice, a man who lives to terrorize me in my moments of respite.

The ghost of his fingertips graze my skin, leaving goosebumps in their wake. A horror I don't want to live.

One that is interrupted by another voice. An authoritative woman with a husky tone sends me spiraling into another vortex of fear.

"Are you there, can we talk?" She's at the door, her knuckles brushing it with a softness that I feel is a lie. Her intentions are not pure. I'm certain of that as I press myself against the cool, wet tile of the shower. It's slippery, and I lose my footing while I try to scramble back from where she calls my name.

A name I rebuke, screaming at her to leave me be as I slip on the floor of the tub. A sudden, bruising fall takes me into darkness.

———

MY MOTHER IS GONE when I wake, in my bed and in a pair of sleep pants that keep me decent. A blush of shame moves over me at the knowledge that she dragged me naked from the shower and placed me into bed after dressing me. It brings me back to childhood. Back to the time when I was weak.

A time I don't dwell on as I take myself to the closet. To find an outfit for the day—a day I dread. One where I will face the halls alone, without Adam.

I think of how I burned his blood in my mother's hearth and I close my eyes, willing it away as I yank on a shirt.

The path out of my room and through the house is one I make on autopilot. Down to the car that I didn't earn, the one that my mother gave me. A relic that lingers after the departure of my father. A cherry red El Camino from an era that passed long before I was born.

It rumbles to life, and the sound is a death knell that fills me with dread as I take the familiar path to the school.

The halls are unchanged—laughter from familiar cliques —and in the middle of all the normal chaos, that parts like the Red Sea, stands Jean. A goddess of retribution that stands still amongst the movement of life, her amber eyes pin me to the spot. A dangerous smile curves across her crimson painted lips, and a shudder moves through me at the memory of the night previous. When she pressed blood-stained lips to mine and pushed the blood of my teammate, of Adam, into me.

Her lips move around words I cannot hear. I try to trace the shape of her mouth, to decipher what she says.

Watch yourself.

Another cold sliver of fear fills my stomach, I'm on the verge of a panic, but a hand slamming down on my shoulder draws me out of the roar of my own blood pounding in my ears.

Braden, too loud and too close, says, "Dude, we gotta talk."

I wonder if he sees the fear that pulls the skin over my face tight.

"What's up?" I hope there's no tremor in my question.

"Adam, man, he texted that he was done covering for me." Braden's face darkens with a rare scowl. His fingers dig into my shoulder, his rage in that grip and I manage to keep from releasing a grunt. Bite it down the way I always do when Braden pushes past a boundary I tried to establish.

"What do you need me to do?" I ask, the question heavy on my tongue. One I have to force off of it with great care, and I hate myself a little more for having asked.

"Meet me at Jeanie Knight's grave at nine tonight."

I glance down the hall, the one where Jean had previously stood. Her dark hair is a veil of night that follows her lithe form as she turns around a corner. Disappearing into the halls. "Why there?"

"No one ever watches that place."

———

NO TRACE of Adam remains in the gloom of night. I look, but not even a hint of his blood remains. As if that creature that Jean shifted into absorbed all that he left behind. A crime without evidence. I don't know if I'm more relieved or horrified.

I have to leave this town.

The one truth I cling to, as I sit near the iron bars of Jeanie's grave. Nothing is disturbed here, but I still feel uneasy. A monster that pushes past the one "known" protection is a beast I don't want to tangle with.

A truth I don't think over for long, my attention is pulled to the crawl of tires over the gravel path of the old entrance. The headlights are off as Braden moves through the overgrowth.

"Did anyone see you?" He asks as he climbs from the car. The features of his face are hard to determine, but I can make out a faint outline.

"No," I say, though I cannot tell him I'm not sure. My

head hasn't been in any of this since the night when Braden raped a girl for all of us to hear.

"Good," he murmurs, going around to the trunk of his car.

"What are you doing?" I ask, suddenly worried for my own wellbeing. Adam is dead—Braden doesn't seem to know that yet and I'm not willing to be the one to tell him. To have him turn his attention on me is a fool's game I'm not willing to play.

"I am making sure we scare his ass so bad he never talks again," Braden says with a steely tone. As he comes back around the car, I hear the clang of metal on metal muffled by a bag.

"What's in the bag?" I'm not sure I want to know, but I'm feeling masochistic.

"Some tools from one of my dad's fun rooms." Braden's father is the adult version of what his son will become. His toys are instruments of horror and there's a rumor that he's paid off a woman or two.

I don't dig too deeply there; I'm not trying to find out more about these people I can't wait to leave.

"What're you planning on doing with them?" I ask, just to know what sort of terrible things to plan for.

"I haven't quite decided," Braden says, voice casual and soft belying the sharp, vile intentions in his words. "Break out his teeth, tear up his throwing arm," a terrible prospect, more horrible than broken teeth. Ruining a throwing arm means never leaving this terrible town.

"All I need is for you to hold him while I do what needs to be done." He continues when I don't say anything. "Good," again Braden takes my silence as compliance.

A text pings on his phone and, after a glance, he says, "Get in the car, it's time to go."

I'm too tired to fight him, and I climb into the passenger seat without question.

He drives us down the familiar road that leads to the school, and I sit there, watching Braden's face as it darkens with each passing mile.

————

THE LOCKER ROOMS are never closed, and Braden opens the door as easily at this hour of midnight as he would in the daylight.

As he holds the door, I glance off into the distance, past the parking lot. When empty it's easier to see all the way to the football field. Illuminated by lights that never go down, I can see a lone dark figure standing at the center yard line. Her dark hair gleams beneath the lights and her eyes glow amber as that smile reappears on her red mouth.

My heart ticks up in my chest.

I hurry inside after Braden. He has his back to me, bending over a duffle bag in the dimly lit locker room, rifling around through the contents.

"We should probably get out of here," I say. Nerves rattling my words.

Braden pauses his perusal of the bag and stands straight before he turns to face me with a surprised expression.

"What?"

"I can't explain, but we gotta get out of here, man. Before she shows up."

"Before *who* shows up?" Braden asks me with a confused frown.

"Jeanie," I hiss. Glancing over my shoulder, as if expecting her to appear through the door.

"Jeanie?" He mocks with a laugh, "That old bitch is a story, Todd. She's not going to show up and kill us."

"Don't say her name," I warn, wondering if that is why she keeps appearing, because I keep calling out her name.

Braden cracks a smile, pressing the hilt of a long knife into my hand. "Hold on tight, Todd, you'll need this when Jeanie comes."

A stillness settles around us, and I know then that Braden shouldn't have tempted fate. She materializes from the darkness. Her body is a cold, white glow in the gloom.

Braden is staring at my face, a rare worry crinkling the skin around his eyes and his mouth. "Todd?"

The scream lurches out of nothing, a devil's call to battle as I watch Jeanie's sharp teeth glisten as she opens her jaw. The first bite causes Braden to stumble back and he moves away from me with the fear of a child being hunted by a bully. He's gone from predator to prey, and I watch, in unmoving fascination, as he screams.

Detachment reigns over me, rooting me to the spot as I watch Jeanie carve words across Braden's chest, the scent of blood fills the room. Cloying and too much as Braden begs for mercy.

She cuts him across the mouth, tearing the corners to widen his mouth.

"Todd," he cries again, while Jeanie cackles.

Her teeth tear at Braden's ear, and she spits his flesh on the floor, "All rapists taste the same, like overpriced shit." She murmurs. Wiping her mouth with the back of her arm before she wanders closer. Moving towards her victim at a slow pace.

"Todd," Braden begs again, staring up at me as he covers his face against Jeanie's final act.

She turns, coming closer to me, with that deranged, blood-drenched smile and I am frozen as she approaches.

Her hands touch mine, warm with Braden's blood, and I shiver as she traces her fingers up my forearm, wrapping them around my wrist.

"Look what you did," Jeanie says to me, but I ignore her and shake my head. "Look, I said," she commands in a sharper tone. When I don't open my eyes she moves her slippery, bloody palm to my cheek, encouraging me to turn my head. I do but I refuse to open my eyes. Terrified of what she will force me to see.

"Open your eyes," she commands when I struggle to peel open my eyelids. "Now." Her fingers dig deeper into my throat.

What I see, as I open my eyes, is a strange, non-corporeal being moving in and out of focus. That's not what frightens me. It's her body, seemingly fused with mine and the murderous look on my face that terrifies me. In my hands is a bloody knife that drips with the blood of Braden's body. Jeanie grins at my side.

"Now you see your true face," she murmurs, bloody lips on mine once more.

"No," I scream and a knock comes against the door to the locker room.

"Todd," she calls and I know that voice, but it's one I refuse to acknowledge, instead I turn to Jeanie. Knowing soon I will be drawn from this hellscape.

"Am I here or is this your idea of self-preservation," Jeanie asks me.

"Go away," I scream, and scream it again and again and again.

Doctor

The man's hands are clasped, fingers squeezing so hard that his skin is white at the knuckles and dark pink at his fingertips. His right knee bounces, a constant movement that fills the silent office with nervous sounds.

"Tell me again," Doctor Mitchell says with quiet authority. Pressing, but maintaining a level of affected empathy—the hallmark of any decent psychiatrist.

Though, if Doctor Mitchell was being honest, he would tell this colleague turned patient to drown himself in the Hudson.

That's not feasible and could result in losing his license, so Doctor Mitchell maintains a facade of patience while he waits for this man to unburden his soul.

A dry swallow works its way down the man's throat—loud in the eerie stillness that settles between them. A gaping divide despite the fact that they sit no more than four feet apart; it feels further to Doctor Mitchell. It always does when he looks into the depths of a depraved soul.

Am I this horrible? This damaged?

These are the things he wonders while he taps the tip of his pin against his yellow legal pad. He never takes notes in these sessions. It was one of his colleague's stipulations.

I'll let you head shrinker me, Darren, but I won't let you take notes or record me.

That, Darren believes, should've been a sign that he didn't need a look into this man's soul.

During these sessions, he cannot bring himself to even think of the man's name.

Giving monsters names makes them real.

That was a lesson Darren's mother once gave, and he's been learning that the hard way for forty years.

"If you don't tell me again, I can't help you," he puts emphasis on the last word. For that was another stipulation. The man across from him, the one twitching on Darren's black leather couch, told him he couldn't speak the man's name.

In here, Darren, I am different. In here I am nameless.

"Todd," he begins with a swallow. A harrowed expression shifting his face, making him appear younger than his distinguished age. Taking him from a grown, middle-aged man, to a youth Darren would not ever want to experience. "Todd haunts my dreams."

"I've noticed," Darren can't help the sarcasm. These sessions always round back to Todd...

To Braden...

To the sister he refuses to name.

Stories that they touch upon, but that this man—this unhealed *boy*—refuses to dive into. There is no healing without self-reckoning. A heavy, self-confrontation, one that this patient refuses. A self-work that this fellow doctor rebukes, and Darren sits baffled that a man can help others heal while being severely damaged himself.

"You don't understand," he whispers, a childish tone dominating the powerful, deep baritone Darren came to expect from his fellow psychiatrist. "They are in me, constantly. They are here." He points to his temple. Finger pressing into the silver hair there. "They never stop, Darren."

"Tell me about what Todd did," Darren commands, firm and insistent.

"I can't…"

"Why?" He asks, needing this man to speak his fears. Darren has a feeling they're rooted in becoming Todd.

"I see him in myself. Constantly…they're there, under the surface and I can feel them in me. Taunting me in my waking hours the way they taunt me in my nightmares."

"Tell me about your sister."

His shoulders are tense. Drawn tight like an over-wound string on a violin, he whispers, "She was his favorite. Todd's love was rooted in violence and, Jea-, uh, my sister, as his favorite was his preferred outlet for his wicked games."

"Did he play these games with you, as well?" Darren has walked his patient close to the revelation before, but he never admits what Darren suspects.

His jaw clenches, Darren watches as his patient's mandible shifts side to side. A motion that causes his teeth to scratch against each other with the same hair-raising sound as nails on a chalkboard.

"I don't want to talk about it," he finally admits, and Darren knows, in his heart, that those words are as good as a confession.

"Tell me about the sister who has become a legend in your mind."

Always a horrific creature of vengeance in the dreams that Darren's patient concocts within sleep. Sometimes he wonders if the sister is even real, wonders if perhaps she is a figment of this man's imagination. One meant to protect the still wounded boy inside of the grown body from a monster Darren has never met.

A monster he would not want to meet, not on his sofa, or in a cell, and certainly not in his own childhood.

"I can't."

"She won't hurt you," Darren soothes, despite his annoyance.

"You don't know that," he growls in return. "She's...dangerous. In ways Todd never was." He's parsing his words, Darren knows evasion when he sees it, but he doesn't fight hard enough with this man.

Cowardice lives in Darren, as well, knowing what lies within this man would mean seeing him every day and knowing that he is guarding the secrets of a kind-faced monster.

That's a liability he should avoid.

The timer goes off, a sharp sound that cuts through the silence with a jarring ring. It would be startling if the alert was not a welcome reprieve.

Man

Darren had been useless, as he expected. It's a disappointment he shoves down as he nods at the doorman of the building. Another bland face that he forgets in his haste to get home.

To check on *her*.

The problem with therapy is that he knows how to lie. He knows what things to hold back, even during those moments when he should be honest.

Vulnerable.

Todd and Braden had killed the vulnerability in him, and the ghosts of their memory continued to haunt him. Reminding him that he was complicit in a lot of their crimes.

The dreams made it worse.

His tormentors came in various decades. Modern or historic. They assaulted him with various color schemes. Bright and bold at times, at others they turn sepia or grayscale. The ghosts of his father and his uncle taunt him with dreams that are silent, then sometimes they are so loud he can't escape the voices when he wakes.

Even now, after the dream about J—*her*—he feels their presence.

The apartment, large for a single man, is bright white. Sterile. Lacking shadows and lacking warmth.

His life is one without attachments. Mostly, it's a world with easily moved parts.

However, there is one locked room in his empty world.

One shadowed room where all the warmth resides.

He moves towards the locked door with purpose, his eyes landing on the princess-themed nameplate that is hung low. At level for the eye of a child.

Daughter. He thinks, and as his blue eyes trace the letters there a strange, unholy smile curves his old mouth.

The handle turns easily, opening with a squeak one he could oil away but there's a devil in him who lives to instill fear. An inborn evil that he is certain was passed from Todd and into himself.

Daughter sits at a decorated vanity dressed in silk garments and a crown. Her eyes meet his in the mirror, fear widening her pupil until her blue iris is nearly devoured. A predatory glee fills the man as he stalks into the room.

"I wouldn't do that," she says with a shrill, desperate voice. Her small body is trying to seem larger, more dangerous than it is. Defensive, because this *Daughter* is new and has yet to learn her place.

"Why is that my darling?" He asks, his voice no longer that scared-childish inflection he used while seated on Darren's couch. Now it is the voice of a monster, one he knows too well, one that sounds like Todd.

In the mirror, he watches as her pale skin drains of color. Sallow is the shade of terror.

"Jeanie Knight," she says to her own reflection. A chuckle leaves him as she says the name again. Leisurely, he stalks closer.

"Jeanie Knight." His body is near the vanity, close enough that he can tell she's wet herself by the scent. As he reaches out a hand to touch the feathery-soft, golden curls on her head, he bends down and grins into the mirror. His own hiss speaking that horrid name, "Jeanie Knight."

A cruel laugh booms from his throat as he tells this child, "No one is coming to save you. Jeanie is just a story."

She stares up at the man with tears falling over young cheeks, and he reaches for her again. His intentions are another vile night of *Play Time*.

Only a creek, as the door hinge moves, gives him a sudden pause.

The child before him, his unnamed toy, smiles. A grin that reminds him of another girl. One more beguiling than any other. A ghost he's constantly chasing.

"Why are you laughing?" He demands of this girl. The one who makes him feel small, foolish, despite her young age.

A giggle leaves her, her mouth twisting with a sinister sneer as she points behind him. The hairs on his nape stand to attention.

Slowly, with his heart pounding, he turns.

There, in the darkened corner of the vibrant room. The one he purposefully decorated with pinks and purples and childish comforts *She* stands. Wearing that damnable prom dress soaked in blood. The one he vividly recalls staring at from beneath the privacy of metal bleachers—hidden with another small girl he had killed. Fearful of her *telling*.

"I told you," Jeanie says as she stalks closer. His feet are rooted to the floor in terror, as she approaches where he stands with a quiet rage. "I told you that when you became a vile man I'd kill you, Adam."

She had. After the last *film* Todd and Braden directed in the family's dingy basement. When Adam and Jeanie had grown *too old* to remain their stars. That was the first time she'd looked at her brother with open hatred.

The first time Adam had been a willing and eager participant.

"Jeanie," he whispers, begging her as he falls down on aged knees. "Please, Jeanie, I won't ever hurt her again."

"Don't you remember?" She whispers, a harsh edge to the words as she drops down in front of Adam. Whisky-colored eyes meeting his, "That's what you said every time when we were growing up. You promised I'd be the only one…and here you are again, brother. Hurting girls in my place."

"I'm sorry," He sobs. Her cold hands are on him, moving through his salt and pepper hair as they make a path to his neck. Her fingers dig into the soft, yielding flesh of his throat while Jeanie whispers against his ear about the sweet salvation that will be Adam's death.

"Not as sorry as you're gonna be," Jeanie replies.

He opens his eyes, finding his nameless daughter. Her blue eyes stare up at him, impassive, as he takes in his newest position in the room. Adam stands on a wooden chair—cold, silk sheets that felt like Jeanie's hands are wrapped around his neck. His hands, though unbound, will not obey Adam's command.

"Darling," he calls to the child, "Help get Daddy down."

She doesn't move. Hatred replaces the usual fear in that gaze.

A chill runs down Adam's spine, as the ethereal form of his darling, *dead* Jeanie moves from behind his chair. She's still in that gown Todd often made her wear. The one soaked with blood and horrors worse than death. The gown he used to make his daughter into his own, perfect mother.

"Please, Jean," Adam begs, straining towards her. "Please, I have to help this girl."

"You've helped her plenty," she replies with a hate-filled hiss. Moments after the words leave her mouth a cruel, satisfied smile curves the soft blue hue of her lips. "Go help someone in Hell."

He hears the scrape of the wood against the floor as the bottom is kicked out from beneath him. Adam's final moment of waking is full of Jean's laughter and his own horrified shout.

Woman

The tip had come from Doctor Mitchell. An anonymous source, but that was a lie, all the lines are equipped with caller ID. Anonymity is an illusion. No one walks away from anything without a trace.

Or so she had believed before they made their way to the Tribeca Tower. Where evil hid beneath the guise of opulence and wealth.

Margaret finds it difficult to feel empathy for the carcass that lies at her boot-covered feet—the body bloated with its orifices full of flies. Details CSU meticulously documents. A body that has decomposed for weeks.

If it was up to me, we would just forget this body to rot.

"Mags," Detective Wilson calls from the other corner of the disturbing room. "Check this out." His long, glove-covered fingers open one of the many strange scrapbooks that are kept in this home.

The office—where Margaret had stood in stone-faced

silence when they got the call earlier that same morning—was lined with wall-to-wall black bookshelves. Each and every spot held a leather bound, black scrapbook. Hundreds, if not thousands, and the first one opened was enough for the Homicide investigator to call SVU.

Margaret doesn't want to look at the pages her partner is going through. Sam's face white with rage as he grits his jaw.

The first scrapbook Margaret had opened in the office was enough to make her long for a lobotomy. To bleach her brain and scrub from it the horrors that lay within those pages.

This scrapbook that Sam holds is much the same. Evil images, torture of the foulest kind, that have little, neatly detailed boxes full of things that document dates, times, descriptions.

"Adam Knight," Sam shakes his head, disgust apparent in his voice as he moves through the album with careful consideration. Trying not to damage what could be important to this investigation, he lands on a page that is full of old newspaper articles about Todd Knight and his half-brother Braden. Horrible, rotten men that were well remembered in a small town about two hours East of this hellish city.

Thirty years have gone and there are still the whispers of their violence that move in hushed tones through old homes, through the small grocery store, and through the school halls followed by delighted giggles.

Margaret recognizes the names from her time at the academy, and from one of her earliest cold case investigations. In that boring time before she moved up from cold cases to SVU.

That particular case Margaret and her old partner had to track down one of Todd's rare, living victims. Mags remembers that woman looked like the old version of what she imagined Todd's daughter Jeanie would look like—*if she had been permitted to grow to adulthood the way my own mother had.*

It wasn't a well-known case, overshadowed by larger cases

that made headlines. In '91 Jeffrey Dahmer eclipsed the deranged girl who killed her tormentors. Jeanie Knight. The Prom Slaughter Queen.

Her grave was pitched in an old county cemetery a couple of hours east—iron bands thrown over top of the plot in the hopes that her spirit would not haunt those who might dare to speak her name. Old superstitions that were implemented by men who feared the power of a woman's rage.

Margaret had been out there, a few months prior, unbeknownst to anyone. She had stood over that rusted iron grate, staring at it with warring emotions while she threw salt and earth upon that dead woman's grave. Jeanie laid beneath the ground, an eternal sprite caught between youth and womanhood. A cautionary tale to Margaret about the evils of men and how they will push a woman into a corner until she comes out of it fighting...only when she does, that woman is labeled *crazy. Insane.*

A danger to the world.

Jeanie Knight—the image of the woman's grave is there, in the scrapbook, and Margaret reads her tombstone, as if it is the first time, for Sam's benefit.

Daughter. Friend. Lover. Mother.

Her golden eyes linger on the word mother, and Sam notices the hard clench of Margaret's jaw.

"That's just weird to think, maybe there's one more devil in this family left." He notes the room around them, "Do you think this is where that child was kept? Do you think Adam took the kid and repeated Todd's torture?"

"You've seen the pictures, Jean died thirty years ago. And that dead little girl in the bed isn't thirty. She's five at most, maybe older if he was starving her for a couple of years." Margaret didn't want to glance to the bed where she knew that small, still fresh body lay posed—as if in sleep. "My guess is that the good doctor Adam found her and brought her here." *Or kidnapped her from some place she wouldn't be missed.*

Considering the number of albums he had in his office, Margaret wouldn't be shocked if there were more victims than this girl. More bodies buried in graves that were only marked in the memory of a dead pervert.

A girl he called *Jean*, according to the nameplate on this bedroom door.

Martin's voice catches Margaret off guard, "Mags, Sam, we've got something over here." Dread is apparent in both of them, by the way they exchange a grim glance.

Martin holds a camcorder up, and Margaret doesn't step closer—unsure if she wants to bear witness to the horrors that Sam moves over to see. He shudders as if this is also wearing on his soul. Not seeing doesn't stop the sounds. Margaret hears a child's small voice shout *no* and she closes her eyes as the girl's pleading grows desperate. Followed by other sounds, and disgusting breathing, she doesn't care to try and name. Then there's more, something wholly chilling as the little girl cries out a name: *Jeanie.*

And again.

And again.

Three times she screams and Sam's eyes flick up to Margaret's. There's no teasing in his expression, just anger and a notable dose of sorrow.

Margaret feels those things too—pity for a girl who died in violence while calling upon the vengeance of a dead woman who became a legend. A god in her own right.

———

MARGARET MAKES her way home at midnight. Known as the witching hour to some. As she opens the slot for her mail, in the apartment's front hall, Margaret's mind lingers on the scrapbook. The one she took out of the office without permission—*to study the evidence* she will claim. Should anyone ask. There are articles Margaret wants to inspect closely. While out from under the watchful gaze of her partner. Sam is a seasoned detective, and a damned good one. He will spot her tells, and Margaret doesn't want to give him the opportunity.

There is a special package with Margaret's name on the front. She holds it with trembling fingers while she reads the *Urgent* and *Confidential* words that are stamped in red ink across the large envelope.

Margaret knew the results the moment she walked into Adam's apartment. She knew the results the moment she first had a hint of doubt.

She knows the results now, as she opens the papers her mother forgot to take out of Margaret's old baby albums. There, in sepia tones, lie cutouts from old papers naming Margaret Jean Knight as a corrupt authority on the raising of children. Equally old articles with Margaret Jean Knight that named the sour-looking old woman in money-hushed abuse cases. Newer articles, hidden in between scrapbook pages, outline Todd's, along with his half-brother Braden's, crimes. Another series of short articles—buried in the pouch with Margaret's hospital birth certificate—were all clipped from a prestigious university's paper. Those all featured a young, visually pleasing Adam Knight. His pictures were faded, as if touched with the pad of an obsessive finger while the details of his accolades, during his journey towards his doctorate, were pristine. Margaret opened the scrapbook that came from Adam's house. Her gloved hands and sterile environment meant that she would leave no evidence of her snooping. Greedily she turned the pages. Searching for articles that matched the ones in her baby book. They were there, more preserved at times, in Adam's files.

Her mother's eerie obsession with a family her mother should have had nothing to do with…

Or Margaret hoped.

A hope that dies a quiet, but painful, death as she turns the pages of Adam's scrapbook.

There is an article, probably the last one in physical existence, of a girl in a dress soaked with blood. Wearing a grin Margaret knows well.

One she seeks as she opens her own scrapbook to compare.

Within the pages of her baby book, Margaret touches the image of her young mother, beaming as the woman holds her newborn in her slim arms. *Perhaps*, Margaret thinks, *it's the job turning me paranoid*. However, she can see too many similarities between her mother—between herself—and the girl beaming up at Margaret in sepia tones. Grinning a deranged, triumphant smile from beneath the lights of a football field, splattered with blood and wearing a childish crown.

A crown Margaret swears she's seen in her mother's closet. Hidden away for as long as Margaret has had memories. *That's not a crown for you.* Her mother used to say.

It's just paranoia. Margaret tells herself-—a mantra that rings through her mind as she reads the name on her birth certificate.

Margaret J. Kentwood.

"Jeanie," she whispers into the stillness of her room.

"Jeanie." Again Margaret says her name, bolder this time.

Then with rage as she hisses that name a final time, "Jeanie."

A brownout darkens the building—for just a second—and Margaret's heart thunders in her chest as her cell phone gives off a shrill ring.

"Hello?" Margaret answers, voice trembling.

"Honey," her mother says, "I had a feeling you needed me."

About the Authors

Marisa Mohi is a writer, tarot reader, and creative coach. She lives in Oklahoma City, Oklahoma with her partner, Chris, and an unruly mutt, Rosie.

https://marisamohi.com/

Kathryn Trattner has loved fairy tales, folk stories, and mythology all of her life. She lives in Oklahoma with her wonderful partner and two very busy children.

https://www.kathryntrattner.com/

Marnie Vinge is a novelist and the creator of the Eerie Okie podcast. She's been writing horror and suspense for over two decades.

https://www.marnievinge.net/

Collette Carmon, a lover of macabre themes and dark romance, has been writing horror, southern gothic, and dark romance for over twenty years.

http://collettecarmon.com/